BUSHWHACKED

"I don't see any likely place for a crossing," said young David Bard. He'd come downriver, far from the wagon train, at the request of the scout, Fast Ed Hernon.

"It quiets down a little further," said Hernon. "Wait and see."

David, in his role as leader of the wagon train, had gotten along smoothly with the rugged frontiersman, and hence had no reason to be suspicious. He was quite unaware of the fierce passion Hernon had conceived for David's intended bride, Edna Sunset.

"All right, if you say so."

They leapfrogged the rocks along the riverbank, until they stood perilously close to the fast-rushing river.

Standing behind Bard, the frontiersman drew one of his heavy Navy Colts. No man in a stunned condition could survive in the cold, swift waters.

He brought the gun butt down in a sudden, crushing arc . . .

The Making of America Series

THE SIXGUN
APOSTLES

Lee Davis Willoughby

A DELL/JAMES A. BRYANS BOOK

Published by
Dell Publishing Co., Inc.
1 Dag Hammarskjold Plaza
New York, New York 10017

Dell ® TM 681510, Dell Publishing Co., Inc.

ISBN: 0-440-08545-4

Printed in the United States of America

First printing—June, 1985

For Kenny Opalsky,
who, like Saint Christopher, was brave enough
to light one candle and not curse
the Darkness. Right on, Kayo.

THE SIXGUN APOSTLES

BOOK ONE

GENESIS:
JOHN BROWN'S BODY

THE HELLFIRE MAN

There was godlessness in the west Virginia air that day. Remorseless, terrible godlessness filling the troubled land as far as the eye could see.

Godlessness, ironically, spearheaded by a man of God.

A Bible-reading, scriptures-quoting demon who knew the Good Book from Genesis to "world without end, Amen." A tall, fierce, flowing-white bearded giant bearing a gleaming rifle and wielding a shining, polished, swift sword. A leader of abolitionists, a fiery advocate of freedom for all men, regardless of station in life or color of skin. John Brown—no name more simple, no man more complex.

He was a legend—"Old Osawatomie Brown"—who had defended Osawatomie, Kansas, from attack by pro-slavery men in 1856. A butcher—he had carved and slaughtered five pro-slavers on the banks of Pottawatomie Creek in the bloody moonlight, his reprisal for the burning and pillaging of Lawrence, Kansas—''Pottawatomie John'' that time. He had married twice and sired a flock of twenty children, had failed in every business venture he had ever undertaken. But now the business of slavery in the United States took all his time and superhuman effort. Death to all men who made slaves of others! The wrath of God was on John Brown's side. He was sure of that. He made good use of the Lord and his Almighty name. Everyone who followed John Brown in the battle against slavery, all his sons and all his cohorts, felt they were the instruments of divine justice. *''Vengeance is mine'' sayeth the Lord*— John Brown said it over and over again. Until it was gospel to all in his wake.

President James Buchanan, serving in the White House in these trying years with North and South divided on the issue of slavery, had chosen a policy of peaceful government. Even with more than half of the slave states already seceded from the Union and the dire threat of a civil war hanging over the land like the sword of Damocles, Buchanan insisted that the letter of the Constitution protected slavery and that the laws must be obeyed. The fledgling United States, still undeveloped beyond the Middle West, where territories, not states, filled out the maps, was in the most crucial stage of its existence. New England was aroused—slavery was God-less. The Lincoln-Douglas debates in Illinois had fanned the flames of public disagreement and discontent. Speculation in western lands and railroads added to the economic panic. The nation was in upheaval. Forces were gathering; the storm was in the wind—it had gone beyond *Does one man have the right to own another man, body and soul?* America's growing pains made it difficult to provide an answer. And President Buchanan's timidity and patience were not for the likes of a man like John Brown, idealist.

He could not, would not, wait. Destiny called him.

The Lord had told him what to do. He had listened.

He would take up arms against this sea of trouble; he would show the way; he would make up the nation's mind for it—he would lead an army out of the wilderness, a force that would grow and build into an unstoppable, relentless, ineluctable legion, marching in the service of God, leading the United States to victory over those who would enslave other men—*Render therefore unto Caesar the things which are Caesar's; and unto God the things that are God's. . . .*

John Brown knew his Good Book. The meaning was all too clear.

He also knew that to make war he needed guns, ammunition. Weapons of all kinds. An army cannot fight simply with words, even though they be true words. Gospel and scripture. *An eye for an eye . . .*

There was a United States Army arsenal at Harpers Ferry in western Virginia. Situated on the Potomac River, just fifty five miles from the nation's capital, Washington, D.C. The tree-covered hills of the Blue Ridge Mountains watch over the Potomac as it meets the Shenandoah River in a wide, sweeping curve. There stood the building which housed the arsenal and armory that John Brown so sorely needed for his war against slavery. A building of wood and stone, weakly garrisoned.

This is what he would take. By force and sheer determination. ·

He would do it with eighteen men. With a prayer on his lips.

And a boy. A ninteen-year-old orphan of great courage.

On the day of October 16th, 1859, Harpers Ferry would fall.

By the dawn's early light.

With the men behind him and the Lord at his side. *Amen!*

The hand of God would never be more in evidence on this blighted land. Glory, glory, hallelujah.

The Truth would go marching on. Jehovah's truth.

John Brown's truth. . . .

Though two years yet remained before a gentle woman named Julia Ward Howe, impressed and touched by her visit to army camps in the Washington of '61, would sit down and pen a stirring hymn to the music of the popular song known as "John Brown's Body," the spirit and patriotic fervor of "The Battle Hymn Of The Republic" was already being forged.

Harpers Ferry sounded the battle cry.

It was to be a tocsin heard throughout the land.

A bellwether of things to come. For all Americans.

A harbinger of war. For Northerner and Southerner alike.

The opening gun of a terrible conflict that would all but destroy the Union forever. By setting brother against brother.

Harpers Ferry was the stuff that the Civil War was made of.

For David Bard, it was the beginning of his life.

There were thunder and lightning and bugle calls in the air—and all the promise of a lifetime of great things, great deeds.

As well as the voice of God. . . .

October 16th was a day of judgment.

For all men, everywhere.

And the flag that fluttered from the pole atop the arsenal at Harpers Ferry, the proud symbol of the United States, the one that bore thirty-one stars, one for each state in the Union, and thirteen stripes, one for each of the original colonies, would not stop John Brown.

He would just as soon shoot at it as look at it.

John Brown's body was preparing to take that last giant step which would precipitate it into the grave of treason, infamy, and madness. A step he would not recall if he could have.

Whom the Gods would destroy they would first make mad.

Brown had read those words a thousand times, but he had never lingered over them to fully find and grasp their meaning. Idealism and self-righteousness blinded him.

All of which boded ill for the morning of October the sixteenth, eighteen hundred and fifty-nine.

HARPERS FERRY AND HADES

There were twenty of them in all.

Twenty renegades feverishly eager to flout flag and country and every law of the land. A motley crew of dissidents and rebels led by the tall, lanky Ohio farmer with the flowing white beard and the high-pitched, nasal voice so given to utterances from the Holy Bible as well as mighty oaths of pure country pithiness. John Brown, clearly the leader of this gang, with two cartridge belts crisscrossing his lean torso as his right hand brandished the curiously short sword that had become his talisman of command. The slouch hat angling across his craggy forehead could not hide the blazing eyeballs in his puritanically grim face. Behind him stalked his followers—four of them his own flesh and blood—sons, the seeds of his loin. Young men, far too weak to rebel against their father's stern wishes— too spineless and purposeless to refuse to accompany him on this mad errand. To seize an arsenal, a building, anything at all that was the property of the United States government, was an act amounting to sedition. High treason, in fact. It did not matter that there was no wartime condition—such an act as this would be punishable by death. A firing squad at first light of morning and no mercy shown.

There was enough unrest in the country with the slavery issue dividing all the states into near armed camps as it was.

But John Brown's followers—the sons, the drifters, the vagrants, the homeless farmers; this ragtag, unkempt band, with no uniformity of dress or costume to mark them—worked their stealthy path down from the tree-covered slopes bordering Harpers Ferry in the morning air. There was a crisp, cool aura to the October day. The weather was just fine. A farmer's day. Good for the crops at harvest time. Yet this was not to be for John Brown and his men.

Rifles and shotguns jutted, sidearms poked, pushing saplings and foliage out of the way, the band moved forward in single file, like Indians on the warpath. No red man ever moved more quietly.

No one spoke.

There was no need to.

The plan of attack had been formulated around the last campfire the night before. Each man knew what he had to do. There was no turning back now. John Brown had committed them all to this daring raid. A raid which he claimed would "stiffen the backbone of those who talk and do nothing. With this one stroke, we will show the country what can be done when Christian men of good will and high purpose set their minds to a thing. The holy war against slavery begins here and now. We need the guns, the ammunitions, the weapons, to be found in that arsenal at Harpers Ferry. . . .''

Harpers Ferry held all of these things. And more.

Stacks of U.S. rifle-muskets, the 1855 model, .58 calibre Colt percussion revolvers, cavalry sabers and swords, bayonets, kegs of black powder, cannon, howitzers, mortars—all of the various military equipment so indispensable to a radical giant who would mount a private army to pursue his own personal goals and objectives. The battle against slavery could be won with guns.

Brown had made each of his followers swear a solemn oath, left hand placed on the worn copy of the Bible that he was never without; thus he had extracted a pledge of loyalty—to the death.

David Bard had taken the oath with all the others.

His heart beating, his hand trembling as it touched the grimy surface of the buckram cover of John Brown's Good Book. The Old Testament. The leader's eyes burned back at him.

"Swear, David Bard."

"I swear."

"Swear that you will remain bound to me and all that I do in the name of the Almighty on this glorious journey. And for all the days to come, you will follow me unto the grave."

"I swear, John Brown. On my mother's and father's graves," David Bard murmured, remembering, his voice thick in his throat. His free hand fairly froze to the familiar barrel of his ancient musket. The selfsame weapon his father had bequeathed to him three long years ago on his deathbed in East Brunswick, New Jersey. Breathing his last breath of life, from a ball taken high in his chest from a drunken soldier on hell-raising leave from Fort Necessity, Pennsylvania, Michael Winship Bard had murmured: ". . . .not much to leave . . . you . . . boy . . . but a man needs a gun . . . in this damn land . . . that's a-growin' so fast. . . ."

Yes, a gun had not been much to leave a growing boy not yet a man. Only that and a clapboard farmhouse covering but three acres with a very poor yield of corn, potatoes, and tomatoes. Ma Bard had been long since dead. The birth of a child, stillborn, had claimed her thin, none-too-strong body when David was a mere colt of nine. And the United States Army had made no restitution whatsoever, much less official apology, for one of its senseless uniforms-on-leave, and a sixteen-year-old boy had lost the poor farm to conniving East Brunswick neighbors who had always coveted Mike Bard's land because of its strategic location, land which soon enough became a produce terminal for farmers all over the territory. What did a mere boy know?

David Bard had cleared out of town long before that fact.

Footloose, heartsore, aimless, all alone in the world. He left East Brunswick hating people, hating the United States Army and all those who wore its blue uniform. Like the peacock feather of legend and story, he went where the wind took him. Down through Pennsylvania, along the Virginia border, up to Ohio, then back down to Virginia again. He supported himself as all vagrants and wanderers do. Working any job he could find, a few days at a time, a month here, two weeks there. Clearing rocks, felling trees, road-paving work, construction of barns and outhouses and farmhouses. The lot. Ditch-digging once, for two weeks, because a wealthy farmer had a fancy idea of irrigating his property. All of this toil did nothing for him except keep his body alive, but it did make that body lean and muscular so that at nineteen the stripling boy was as rawboned and strong as any man might want to be. And yet his soul and mind still harvested a bitterness that would not go away. From such troubled soil bitter plants will grow—and John Brown materialized out of the darkness, ready for the plucking. Fire-eating, heaven-and-hell-invoking John Brown.

When David Bard heard him breathing fire and brimstone in one of his many fiery tirades in an open cornfield in Richmond, the die was cast. David had never heard such stirring words, nor had any man ever gotten exactly right to the heart of what he was feeling. He had always suffered somehow, watching black people being treated like something less than human—he became a John Brown zealot on the spot.

He had missed Brown's glory in the defense of Lawrence, Kansas, against the attack of pro-slavery forces. He had not been with Brown on the Pottawatomie Creek massacre expedition. But he was to be on time for Harpers Ferry, thank the Lord. His first genuine baptism of fire with Old Osawatomie Brown. *This is the Lord's work, lad* . . .

John Brown had become the father he had lost.

The family he had never known.

Small wonder that he would take all that the man said as gospel and do anything such a man would ask him to do. The United States and its flag meant nothing to a nineteen-

year-old boy who had been abused and disserviced by that
country and flag.

A man who had served under Old Glory had killed his
father.

And he had lost the loving care and concern of Frances
Hepburn Bard long before he could appreciate her worth
and what she truly had meant to him. The woman who
used to read to him as a child—there by the candlelight—
and the fireplace—*God bless Mama and Papa and me and
help me to be a good boy* . . .

John Brown's thorny hand came down on David Bard's
shoulder.

His eyes were not quite sane in the glowing firelight of
the campsite. "By the eternal! I'm glad you're with us,
David."

"So am I, John Brown."

It was a moment. One that David Bard was certain he
would remember all the rest of his natural life.

And now it was October the sixteenth.

Dawn. The flag flapping briskly in the morning air.

Clouds moving slowly against a blue, serene sky. A
pale sunlight.

The turrets and walls of Harpers Ferry upthrust against
the pastoral backdrop of tree-lined hills. Nothing and nobody stirred.

The small, intense band of twenty men wended its way
down, circling the forested trees, guns and weapons at the
ready, scarcely snapping a twig or making a dry leaf
crackle in protest. No bird called out.

History stood still, awaiting the next moment. Holding
its breath.

The one that would bring sensation, infamy, and disgrace.

And yet give the world the name of John Brown, Abolitionist, for all time, and history, to come.

And cast the first long, dreadful shadow that would ultimately culminate with that terrible conflict known as the Civil War.

The Potomac River crawled lazily toward its juncture with the Shenandoah as John Brown and his band moved toward the high structure that housed the arsenal and armory of the United States government at Harpers Ferry, Virginia. A lone blue-uniformed sentry patrolled sleepily.

Destiny stood but a thousand yards away now.

John Brown and his men rushed to meet it.

David Bard, too.

He was the last man in the long line of twenty infiltrators in the environs of the arsenal. John Brown had ordained it that way. The youngest man on the raid should go last and serve as rear guard lookout. So David was alone, bringing up the rear with John Brown himself in the vanguard. Like a shepherd leading his flock out of the wilderness. Tall, imperious, proud—defiant. The guidon for glory.

As well as his plan was for this unexpected assault on a U. S. Army position. Seize the arsenal, then confiscate all weapons and flee back into the safe shadows of the Blue Ridge Mountains to set up a fortified stronghold from which he could continue the battle against Mother Slavery— damn the bitch goddess!

Even young, inexperienced David Bard saw the wisdom of such thinking. Why, if the national government wouldn't do something about slavery, great men like John Brown could—and would.

Now, his step quickened, his heart yet hammering in the
stillness surrounding the vicinity of the arsenal. Ahead of
him he could see all the others, moving forward swiftly, at
a half-crouch, on running feet, weapons to the fore. He
clutched his own piece so tightly he was sure he was
leaving his print on the stock and barrel. Pa's old gun. An
ancient muzzle-loader dating back to the Revolutionary
War. Yet it had served the Bards well for hunting game.
Deer, pheasant, turkey—and now its muzzle would shoot
down men, if need be.

A pulse in David's throat leaped. He had never killed a
man.

Everything was so still and calm. Yet the air was alive
with tension. The very trees seemed to incline toward the
arsenal, leaning with the twenty human beings stretching
out toward its facade. The lone sentry, pacing in a very
unmilitary fashion at his post, was like a figure painted on
a landscape—solitary, dominant, statue-like.

Now, suddenly, a bird trilled from a nearby elm tree.
Another answered from the right. Mockingbirds, thought
David—they sound like mockingbirds—*listen to the mock-
ingbird, listen to the . . .*

Up ahead of him, one of the band, one of John Brown's
sons—it looked like Caleb Brown—in the morning half-
light, abruptly raised his rifle on high and began to pump
frantically. Like a man in dire need of aid of some kind.
But it was a signal, of course—it had to be! For quickly,
seemingly with one mind, John Brown's stealthy band rose
as one man, straightening erect, and pounded forward,
closing ranks, weapons pointed dead ahead. The unforgettable figure of John Brown, white beard flowing in the
morning breeze, swung aloft the peculiar short sword, his

symbol of leadership. The very sword with which he had helped hack to death the three male members of the Doyle family outside their farmhouse at Pottawatomie Creek in the bloody moonlight. And two more helpless pro-slavers, Wilkinson and William "Dutch Bill" Sherman were savaged by that blade before the break of dawn of the next day. *An eye for an eye and a tooth for a tooth.*

David Bard swallowed nervously and began to run, too.

No one had fired a shot yet, and no one had called out or yelled, but the band of twenty raiders was sweeping forward like an avenging tide. Three hundred yards, two hundred—the structure that housed the arsenal loomed larger still.

And still the dawdling, inattentive, blue-uniformed, armed sentry had not seen the approach of the human tide. Nor heard them.

Now came the moment that comes to all men. The single instant in their lives when a turn to the left or to the right charts that man's journey on this earth for all his time to come. Such a moment arrived for David Bard. One that he had absolutely no choice in. Fate, destiny, or chance alone—the happening was inescapable.

From somewhere behind him, rough hands came out of nowhere, encircling him, squeezing him, bearing him to the hard-packed earth just fronting the forest of trees which perimetered the clearing on which the arsenal building stood. David went down—stunned, shocked, caught completely off guard.

The heavy figure that bore him to the ground was weighty, formidable, smothering him in a brutal vise of manpower. The musket fell from his surprised fingers. The tableau of the advancing raid, John Brown and all the others, was lost to his vision. Now he saw only the overhead trees, the blue sky, the white clouds, the pale ball of sun. Then there was no time or thought for anything else but self-preservation. Whoever or whatever it was that had picked jim off at the end of the advancing line was now trying to finish him off. The silvery gleam of a knife blade darted upward as a vicious, bony knee tried to pin him to the ground, as if he were a hog trussed for slaughter. And a bearded blur of a face grimaced down at him in a frozen leer from under the bill of a foraging cap. With an accompanying grunt of words, strange words: "Hold still, sonny. This'll take but a minute." The tone was coarse, drunken. A heady sour stench of alcohol fumes fanned down at him. His stomach churned.

Dimly, almost faintly, from far off, a shot thundered. Then another and another. Someone was shouting at the top of his lungs. It sounded much like John Brown's high-pitched, nasal voice. The world reeled. Earth, trees, sun, sky, clouds, and the man above him. The silver blade high overhead arced down. David Bard forgot all else but that knife and reacted instinctively. Like a trapped animal.

His terrified eyes had already found and stored all the fleeting impressions of a few seconds. His assailant was a soldier. The blue uniform, the boots, the chevrons, were unmistakable. As slovenly and disheveled as they were. A Federal trooper had ambushed him!

The wicked knife descended as the soldier growled fiercely.

David galvanized, bringing both legs upward in a swinging kick, even as his desperate hands closed about the wrist of the knife-hand. Within flying seconds the entire encounter changed. And the soldier, whoever he was, had obtained more than he had bargained for. The ensuing struggle was now truly life-and-death.

David's boots, worn, scuffed hand-me-downs, thudded into the attacker's stomach. The knife's descent veered sharply to the left. The man shifted to one side, and David, hanging on, followed. Soon both men were locked together, rolling furiously, kicking, clawing. Their combined weight found a knoll, reached it and rolled over the obstacle. There was a fold in the earth, and the combat which had begun beneath a cluster of elms now attained a rolling, twisting, turning formation. Like two dogs locked in animal heat, the combatants turned end over end, landing a full thirty yards from where the fight had begun. And through all the grunting and squirming and exertion of physical struggle, far-off sounds punctuated the still of the morning. A fusillade of rifle shots, then a bugle's loud, clear, clarion voice wafted from the clearing and the direction of the arsenal. The raid was fully under way. As was David's hand-to-hand death fight with a man he had never met or seen before.

The foraging cap had long since fallen from the soldier's head. David's slouch hat had joined it somewhere back there. The bugle's sound cut off abruptly. Hoarse shouts filled the air. And then all sounds and impressions of the raid receded. And there was only the here-and-now. The terrible present.

Somehow, the knife had disappeared too, and the burly, heaving figure in his arms was pressing both coarse, callused hands about his unprotected throat. The fingernails dug in. Flashes of white-hot pain ignited David's brain. He threshed, punched, lashed out, feeling the awful compression of his chest, the search for breath being denied him. A vicious,

gloating sound reached his ears. Through a rapidly building haze before his eyes, he sensed, knew, that he was
losing this battle. That there was hardly enough time left to
rally before he was choked to death. The man brutalizing
him was a big man, fully two hundred pounds, and that
extra weight, tewnty-five pounds more than David's lean,
muscular length was making the difference. Desperately,
recharged with death so near, David Bard did the only
thing left to do. Instinctively, reflexively, such as any
animal would, caught in a merciless vise of brute force.

He gambled. He forgot the hands at his throat. He
dropped his own.

And brought them, clenched togther, in a bony, hard-
knuckled blow, directly into the crotch of the man above
him. There was a howl of sheer agony as his two-handed
thrust pounded home. The choking fingers slackened and
released him. He did not wait. Gasping, coughing, he
pawed at the ground blindly, felt his hands close over the
haft of the big knife. There was nothing more to think
about. Still more dead than alive, he brought the weapon
upward in a stabbing, slicing motion. Another half-choked
blurt, a low scream from the man before him. He thrust
again and again, until suddenly he was completely free of
danger. He staggered erect, the knife still clenched, unsee-
ing, heedless of the red blood which now engulfed its long
blade. He barely saw the kicking, convulsing figure before
him, turning over on the soft green ground of the forest.

Heart pulsing like a dozen drums, head throbbing with a
thousand hornets, David Bard tottered away. Wanting to
get as far as possible from the evidence of his own grisly
handiwork.

Wanting desperately to get back where he belonged.

With John Brown and the others taking the arsenal at
Harpers Ferry in a surprise attack. He was bleeding pro-
fusely from the face, but he did not know that, either. He
knew very little at that particular moment, save that he was
alive and that he had most certainly killed a man. A
Federal soldier—a noncommissioned officer of some kind.
Dimly, memory of corporal chevrons on burly arms flashed
in his mind.

He had lost all sense of direction, though the daylight
had lengthened and now the entire panorama, the landscape, was bathed in pure morning light. The horizon with
its rolling promontories and slopes, the Blue Ridge Mountains, seemed a hundred miles away.

And then came the topmost pinnacle of unreality and
wonder.

From a mere five yards away, the dying corporal, one
Raymond Zimmerman, bleeding to death from three fatal
stab wounds in the stomach, propped himself on one el-
bow, took wavering, unsteady aim at the young man reeling in circles before him, and got off one last shot with his
service pistol. A Colt revolver. Even as he fired, the
corporal gave one last convulsive shudder and died face-
down on the green earth. David Bard would never know
that Zimmerman, a drunken bully on two-days leave from
Harpers Ferry, was fond of having a last bottle by himself
in the woods before reporting for duty. The Bowie knife,
for that is what it was, was strictly illegal sidearms for a
member of the Federal Army. But none of that mattered
now.

The last shot, a .32 calibre ball of lead, found its mark.

A red-hot poker flash of agony lanced through David
Bard's left shoulder. This was the ultimate in pain. The

force of the ball spun the young man around, sent him off once more on a dizzy tangent. With all sense of direction lost, with every muscle and fiber of his being tumulting with shock and weariness, David stumbled, half-dead through the woods. Careening into the boles of thick trees, cruel saplings tearing at his exposed face. A red haze was lowering before his eyes. Before him, the terrain tilted crazily, the trunks of the elms dancing a weird waltz; the vast green of the forest, still not yet completely yielding to the enforced nudity of the oncoming winter months, mocked him.

He was like a child again, alone in his tiny bedroom, caught up in a monstrous nightmare from which only the appearance of his beloved father and mother could save him. But they were both dead, and that was so long ago and he was not a child. . . .

He felt consciousness leaving him, his nerves ebbing into a paralyzing numbness; all of his senses and faculties slowed, deadened. Corporal Zimmerman had given him the beating of his life.

He floundered forward, legs dragging, arms sagging.

His head rioted; his skull wanted to separate itself from his shoulders. The universe darkened; the blue sky dimmed. The white clouds blackened. The sun waned. The air grew dense and heavy and insufferably warmer. He lurched onward, pushing feebly at the saplings and branches slapping at his face.

He had lost his way, completely.

Now he was on his knees, crawling . . . in the opposite direction from that which he and John Brown and the others had come. Away from the target of that day. Away from Harpers Ferry and the all-important arsenal of weapons.

Destiny, fate, the gods, had taken him by the hand.

And led him from the path of self-destruction and infamy.

When he finally collapsed, loss of blood, agony, and total weariness of limb claiming all that was left of his consciousness, he was fully a mile and a half from the point where John Brown had massed his followers for the raid on Harpers Ferry and its arsenal. There was no longer any chance to hear anything.

History and Shame were made that October day.

And only the grace of God had kept a nineteen-year-old youth from going down with all the others.

To death and perdition.

And unhallowed memory.

THE HAND OF JEHOVAH

There was a wagon in his nightmare.

A covered wagon.

The kind of wagon his father had once told him was a Conestoga wagon, named for the Pennsylvania town where it was first built before the American Revolution. The early settlers had used this huge contraption to move their goods and belongings, and families, across the Allegheny Mountains as they searched for new land in the undiscovered country. The great unknown West.

He had seen so many of them as a child growing up in New Jersey, and now, in this nightmare, never had one looked so vivid and real. Bigger than a mountain. A Rocky Mountain.

Pa had called Conestogas "the ships of the prairie," like everyone else had, and David Bard had thought it a good name for such a thing—it did look like some fancy Yankee clipper.

Both ends of the wagon were built higher than the middle. There was a white canvas roof, high and rounded, as spotless as good milk. Four iron wheels with broad rims that prevented bogging down in the mud moved the contraption. That and four or six horses for pulling, to either side of the wagon tongue. The Conestoga of David Bard's nightmare was drawn by four horses.

The wagon stood now, poised on a high, winding road, its identifiable outline framed against a dark sky with skeletonlike trees reaching up to the heavens. The horses were standing like stone figures, looking neither to the right or left, but dead ahead. There was a man and a woman in the nightmare, too. Such a man and such a woman as he had never seen in all his born days.

The man was tall. Incredibly tall.

A wide-brimmed hat with a conical crown and a black frock coat draping his length. Long dark trousers encased his legs. A white shirt and a black tie. And yet this was as nothing compared to the face of the man. A hawk nose jutted from a countenance that was all bronzed like a seaman's. Great white teeth gleamed from a veritable cascade of flaming red hair that triangulated in a pointed beard reaching down to the man's collarbone. And the eyes—in the nightmare they were like two whirling pools of dark fire. They seemed to see right through a body—David Bard blinked.

The man could have been John Brown. Or his image.

And the woman!

Girl, really.

She was tall, also, and her figure, mounted in a flowing

skirt and an apron of sorts, with shoulder straps barely containing the full swell of a ripe bosom, stood to one side of the black-suited giant. But it was her head that was most memorable.

David Bard had never laid eyes on shoulder-length hair, unadorned by combs or ribbons or braids of any kind, which fell so freely down a woman's body and that had all the rich color and silkiness of freshly ripened maize. Nor had he ever beheld two eyes of cornflower blue looking at him from a curved face of unblemished smoothness and tawniness of skin. The girl's nose and mouth were like something he had seen in those pretty pictures in that magazine Ma made Pa send for in the mails—*Godey's Lady's Book*—but he had never dreamed such females ever existed. He had never seen a woman who looked like this in East Brunswick. But now—in his nightmare, or was it a dream, truly?—here was the upturned nose with the delicate pinch of the nostrils, the mouth shaped like a Cupid's bow, red and sweet. And kissable.

The lips parted now; the cornflower-blue eyes melted with pity and compassion, as if the girl were saddened by the sight of him. The tall, black-suited giant at her side was shaking his head grimly. All three apparitions, the wagon and horses, the man, the woman, began to blur and blend before David's eyes.

"Look at him, Edna. Another sinner. A godless youth—"

"Oh, Martinius—he's hurt—he needs help."

"Yes, he's hurt—from carousing, wenching, liquoring himself up—another black sheep, by the look of him."

"No, Martinius—he has been set upon—MARTINIUS!"

David Bard heard no more than that. The woman had screamed.

The nightmare, or dream, had ended for him.

He tipped back into the world of unconsciousness, falling in a dead faint before the oncoming giant and his female companion.

He was never to remember his amazing odyssey from the scene of his self-defense murder of Corporal Raymond Zimmerman. How, half conscious, half dead, he had fumbled and staggered across country, miles from the site of Harpers Ferry, until the sounds of horse and wagon, squeaking wheels and the whicker of horses, had brought him out of the dense forest to the roadside. He had spent the last four hours semi-conscious—only the will for survival and the inner strength of his young body pushing him on. Great thirst and a greater hunger had made him delirious. And the loss of blood had finally done him in.

Nor would he ever truly remember his first encounter with this man and this woman. This strange couple from out of the fog. And doubts and confused impressions of the raid on Harpers Ferry.

Martinius Rheinbeck.

And Edna Sunset.

The circuit rider and his apostle.

Traveling toward their commission in Kentucky. The little town of Horsefall, planted in the last valley just before the Cumberland River, about twenty-five miles south of Gate City, as the crow flies. A new settlement had grown up far from its mission, and someone was needed to bring the Word, to carry it on.

Religion had moved westward, too, along with the people who sought new lands and new freedom from the overcrowded East. Whether Catholic or Protestant, men and women and children needed their gods. The pioneer life was hard enough as it was.

But David Bard knew none of this, much less cared, as he fell into the coma which had been coming on for half of his terrible waking hours that crowded, fateful October day.

Martinius Rheinbeck and Edna Sunset could have been mere figments of his imagination. Phantoms conjured up by delirium.

But they were not, of course. They were real enough.

They were merely Good Samaritans whom the Lord had placed in his path on his journey to the Great Beyond.

As he was to learn, all too soon.

". . .O my God, I am heartily sorry for having offended you and I detest all my sins because of your just punishments, but most of all because they offend you, my God, who are all good and deserving of all my love. I firmly resolve with the help of your grace to sin no more. . . ."

The words, the familiar words, though a shade different from the ones his Catholic parents had taught him, came to him faintly. Very faintly, piercing through a waterfall of noise and thunder. There was a great roaring in his ears. He struggled to come awake. To hear the words properly—the voice that spoke the words was deep, fervent, and somehow reassuring. He was almost lulled, like a child being read aloud to so as to achieve sleep.

". . .glory be to the Father and to the Son and to the Holy Spirit . . . as it was . . ."

He strained, feeling the effort. All of him ached. His face felt on fire. As if it had been scraped clean with a file.

". . . in the beginning . . . is now and ever shall be . . ."

The voice was somewhere above him. Bathing his hearing like a salve for all his hurts. The words calmed him, somehow. He no longer strained or squirmed for consciousness. The voice with all its resonant power, and the lovely words, soothed him.

". . . *world without end, Amen.*"

He drifted off, falling into a deep untroubled sleep now.

He somehow sensed safety and protection, knew inwardly and instinctively that some God-fearing man had spoken over him the Act of Contrition—the prayer he had known all his life because Frances Hepburn Bard had taught it to him when he was old enough to speak. He had even heard John Brown utter those powerful words in that open cornfield in Richmond, getting the crowd of his listeners to fall to their collective knees as bareheaded, hat in hand, he looked to the heavens and beseeched the Almighty to listen as he spoke the Protestant variation of the immortal prayer.

David Bard slept like the child he had once very much been.

His body was an angry battlefield, but his mind was a peaceful bower of safety in a wilderness of confusion. He soared aloft.

He never heard Edna Sunset murmur: "Do you think he will die, Martinius? He's lost a passel of blood."

"No, Sister Edna. He will not. *Yea,* though he's cut all over and bruised like a gored bull with that wound in his shoulder, our young warrior is constructed as sturdily as a hickory tree. As fine a specimen of green manhood as I ever did see. Behold a Samson."

"Do you reckon he's a bad man?"

"There's time enough to learn that when he's ready to

do some talking to us on the subject. For now, it's between him and the good Lord and that's all there is to that.''

''Well, we've done just about all we can for him, haven't we?''

''Amen to that, Sister Edna,'' Martinius Rheinbeck intoned with the assurance of a man who has said that phrase many times. ''Now, see to the horses. We must not forget the poor dumb beasts even as we tend the needs of our less fortunate fellowman.''

''Yes, Martinius.''

Martinius Rheinbeck stared down at the recumbent form of David Bard as Edna Sunset dismounted from the wagon to see to the horses. They had dutifully fashioned a bedlike arrangement for the injured young man in the interior of the wagon. Sister Edna had washed the young man's face with cold water from the nearby creek and Martinius Rheinbeck himself had explored the left shoulder, gratified to find no bullet there. The ball had obviously passed through. Beyond the multiple scratches and bruises on the young colt's face and throat, where one could still see the vicious traceries of cruel, raking hands, there was no earthly reason why the young rip should not recover. A night's rest and some of Sister Edna's healing potato soup with black bread should bring him around in no time at all. The young man was a riddle, though.

There was nothing about his ordinary dress of cotton trousers, woolen jacket, and work shirt to mark him apart from any other man. The scuffed boots had seen much better days. More curiously and not at all likely, the pockets of the boy's clothes contained not a single thing. No papers or cards—not even a letter from home to tell

who he was. Martinius Rheinbeck could not know that it
was John Brown's explicit orders that none of the raiders
on Harpers Ferry should carry any form of identification at
all. He had planned the surprise attack with all the military
efficiency and cunning of a spy. But Martinus Rheinbeck
did not know and did not care—and would not have
cared—about any of all that. Even as he studied the sleeping youth beneath him, the red triangular beard was nodding approvingly.

Yes. Certainly. Why not? Surely the hand of Jehovah
was in evidence here. The Lord did move in mysterious
ways his wonders to perform. . . .

Martinius Rheinbeck had great need of a young man as
sturdy as an ox, by the look of him, for this long, arduous
journey to Horsefall, Kentucky. The road was long and
hard. There was much to be done to navigate the trail
successfully, and it would benefit both Sister Edna and
himself immensely to have another hand on the trek. A
man who could chop wood for the fire, fetch water for the
horses, and also help fend off any attacks by Indians, road
robbers, and all sorts of troublemakers and hell-raisers.
Yes, indeed. A certain gift from the Almighty. Time
enough later to find out who exactly and what precisely
this wounded young buck was. Or had been.

In this troubled day and dangerous age one more pair of
hands and legs and eyes to do God's work was a blessing
of the highest order. Martinius Rheinbeck, for all his
religious fervor, was a practical man. And the last one to
look a gift horse in the eye.

Yet he had never been quite sure of that old axiom. Not
truly.

Had the Greeks looked *their* Trojan horse in the eye,

they would certainly have avoided the fall of Troy—and all the resultant woe.

Martinius Rheinbeck chuckled deep in his chest and set the paradox aside. He too dismounted from the Conestoga to see about the arrangements for supper. It was late afternoon now, the sun going down in the west, dipping behind the low-lying range of mountains. There was a fine cool tang to the October air. No threat of rain at all.

He had knowledge of many things, being a well-read man, everything from the Bible to William Shakespeare to the novels of James Fenimore Cooper and Nathaniel Hawthorne, but he had no way of knowing what had happened that historic day. Civilization was distant.

Some thirty miles to his rear, John Brown and his band of eighteen raiders had overcome the small militia at Harpers Ferry and captured the old arsenal. He had taken prisoners; there were dead and there were wounded, but the news was going out all over the country. By telegraph, by stagecoach, by horseback rider, by word of mouth.

Harpers Ferry was in the hands of John Brown and his band.

Old Osawatomie Brown, the radical abolitionist of the day. Defying the U.S. Government, the pro-slavers, and even God.

A mad act, a treasonable move, punishable by death.

And the far-off, dim rumblings of greater, more terrible things to come sounded in the heavens. Martinius Rheinbeck did not hear them. He was a man of God. As such, Christian thoughts alone were his.

As well as the wounded young man in a healing sleep in the schoonerlike interior of the Conestoga wagon. One David Bard.

But neither man could know at that particular moment how star-crossed both their destinies were. A great road lay ahead of them.

Nor could Edna Sunset, with her eyes of cornflower blue.

The three of them had come together miraculously on the trail toward Kentucky. They had been set in each other's path by the hand of God: Jehovah, the Lord, Yahweh, the Almighty, the Father—Buddha, Tao—whatever name you called him, His will be done.

Men like Martinius Rheinbeck saw to that.

The fifteenth President of the United States received the awesome news of John Brown's spectacular raid on Harpers Ferry late in the afternoon of that very day. James Buchanan was a bachelor, the only national leader the country was ever to know who lived his tenancy in the White House without a First Lady. But Buchanan, who at sixty-six had succeeded his fellow Democrat Franklin Pierce to the greatest seat in the land, was a warm, friendly human being, whose birth in a log cabin in Stony Batter, Pennsylvania, had always kept him cognizant of his humble beginnings. With the nation already in upheaval over the slavery question, he, probably more than anyone else in his Cabinet, realized and dreaded the consequences of Brown's rash act.

He acted without hesitation. Without a moment's remorse.

Concealing his agitation from the concerned members of his staff who had brought him the news, he issued immediate orders and instructions for the army to respond to the threat of John Brown's act of insurrection. And anarchy. An insurrection which must be put down. A platoon of

United States cavalrymen, plumed hats flying, sabers clattering, set off at a full gallop for Harpers Ferry, Virginia. At their head rode a handsome, erect, square-shouldered officer-in-charge who had made quite a name for himself in his days at West Point and with subsequent military achievements. A colonel who chanced to be in Washington when news of Brown's raid reached Buchanan.

Colonel Robert Edward Lee would lead the reprisal on John Brown. With him, and behind him, rode Lieutenants George Armstrong Custer and J.E.B. Stuart. And twoscore seasoned fighting men.

History was truly in the making that October of '59.

And John Brown had triggered the whole thing.

With one wave of his terrible swift sword.

And a fierce cry of *"Charge!"*

The nation was struggling to survive once more.

THE PREACHER AND
THE ANGEL

Rock of Ages, cleft for me,
Let me hide myself in Thee;
Let the water and the blood,
From Thy riven side which flowed,
Be of sin the double cure,
Cleanse me from its guilt and power. . . .

The woman's sweet, high, lyrical voice, singing the
hymn that was perhaps the most rendered by Christian
people of America, awakened David Bard from a sleep
which had lasted all of sixteen hours. He had slept pain-
lessly, easily, his body yielding to the healing powers of a
calm so sorely needed. The gentle rocking and swaying
motion of the big wagon had done the rest. Not even an
occasional sinkhole and bump in the roadway that jarred
the four-wheeled Conestoga could shatter David Bard's
sleep. Martinius Rheinbeck's sure-footed horses, veterans

of a thousand such roads, were as canny as any mountain goats traversing a rocky hillside. The journey had been a smooth one thus far. And the singing of the woman with the long, long hair and the blue, blue eyes was like some lullaby sung by a loving mother. David Bard opened his eyes, blinking against a morning light. The bright splash of sunlight, so different from the darkness of his last moments before unconsciousness, was blinding.

But total recall came to him almost instantly.

John Brown, the raid, the drunken soldier, the staggering flight to safety, the materialization of a tall giant and a beautiful girl—the huge prairie wagon—his eyes sought them now so that his brain could reaffirm what he remembered, could separate dream from reality. He did not have too far to look.

Without moving his head, he could see their backs before him, up front, at the reins of the wagon. The man's wide-brimmed, conical hat topped the impressively broad-shouldered, immense-sized body. Beside him, the woman was like some shapely statue. The long flaxen hair trailed neatly down her firm back. She was humming now, no longer singing the words, and it was such a sweet sound that David lay where he was, letting the melody waft over him. He felt stiffened and sore, but there no longer was any sense of pain. The youth of his body was responding to the healing sleep. That and whatever his two Good Samaritans had done to speed up the process. There was now no more time to think of John Brown and Harpers Ferry. There was so much more to learn—such as where were these two good people taking him? That was one thing he had to know.

"Good morning," he ventured feebly and was surprised to hear how faint and uncertain his own voice was.

The wide-brimmed hat turned; the long-haired back did too—and their two unforgettable faces were looking at him. For a moment he was taken aback. Martinius Rheinbeck's eyes were grimly suspicious though grudgingly cordial, and the woman's compassionate face was more breathtaking than ever. The cornflower-blue eyes were startling, seen so close. And the bright sunlight continued to wash into the interior of the wagon, as though the sun was at its high noon zenith.

"Well, up and about, are you, son? Good. We have much to talk about. How are you feeling?" The words boomed back at him. Martinius Rheinbeck's voice had a carrying quality, as though he would never be able to whisper. The woman touched his arm gently.

"Lower your voice, Martinius," she murmured. "Please— he still looks plumb tuckered out."

Martinius Rheinbeck chuckled. "Take the reins, Sister Edna. I would talk with our black sheep. He will live. The Good Lord has given him the constitution of an ox—well, young man, can we palaver for a spell? There is much to settle between us."

David did not understand. "I'm much obliged—to you both—but if you're talking about money, I'm afraid—"

"Don't be afraid," Rheinbeck scowled, the smile leaving his bearded face as he handed the reins to the woman and clambered into the rear of the wagon, moving deftly, for all his size, off the platform. Edna Sunset shifted her position to the center of the seat and snapped the reins to give the horses the feel of a new driver. She kept her eyes on the roadway, not turning at all, but David knew she would hear all that passed between him and Martinius Rheinbeck.

There was a low wooden stool by his pallet, and the bearded man took this, moving aside a large wooden crate which was unmarked and securely nailed. The wagon's interior also held barrels, David could now see, and no end of supplies. Sacks of flour and cornmeal, canned goods, a brace of shotguns and boxes of ammunition. But there was no time to see more. The tall giant was staring down at him now, his impressively patriarchal face a study in purposeful resolve—and barely a foot from David's own. The hawk nose was dismaying.

"I am Martinius Rheinbeck. The angel is Sister Edna Sunset. We are instruments of the Lord. Spreading the Good Book and its words where we can. We are making straight for Horsefall, Kentucky. Having come from the godless environs of Roanoke. Where they still put the black man in chains and treat him as the dirt of the field. We could do little there in God's name. However, there is a settlement where we are needed—that is where we shall go. It is my sworn duty as an ordained minister of the Church. We are Protestant, son, but we recognize all men and all faiths as the children of the Almighty. Now, have you got all that or shall I say it once more?"

David shook his head slowly.

Martinius Rheinbeck grunted, almost in approval. The swaying wagon seemed to rock in time with his pronouncements.

"Now, you came to us from out of the blue. Battered, bruised, a pistol ball wound in your shoulder. We could guess as to your identity and station in this life, but we will not. It is for you to confess, to tell us. We share our

bread and soup with you and all that we possess and ask
nothing in return from you but the truth. Will you tell us
that, my boy? It is not too much to ask for saving your
life.''

Again David shook his head, but he was unable to
speak.

The woman had not turned or moved from her steering
of the wagon. The road had curved and a low grade was
causing the pace to slacken. He could hear the drawn
horses snorting with exertion.

Martinius Rheinbeck laid a hard-knuckled hand on David's knee. Even through the coarse thickness of a heavy
blanket, he could feel the strength in that hand. Rheinbeck
wore no pistol or sidearm of any kind. It was as if he
scorned weapons. As if he sensed the power of his own
words. Despite the brace of shotguns stacked in the wagon.

"Finally, son, I tell you this. I have no kith or kin but
dear Sister Edna. She is like a daughter to me, and there is
no lust in my heart for her, though she is the most beautiful creature I know. She is an orphan of nineteen. Her
good parents were taken from her in an Indian raid on
Cooperstown many years ago. She is bound to me by God
and the Good Book and is of great assistance to me in
spreading the Word." Rheinbeck sat back on the low stool
and anchored a hand on each knee. "There. Now you
know all there is to know about us. It only remains for you
to tell us about yourself. Then I will tell you what I have
planned for you. Jehovah has placed you in our path for a
reason. I am as sure of that as I am of the snow falling in
the winter. Speak, my boy, you are with good people who
will understand and forgive, if there is forgiving to be
done. It is the way of the Lord. Amen to that.''

The torrent of words had fallen on David's ears like a waterfall. Martinius Rheinbeck had obviously held nothing back. These were preacher-folk, just like John Brown, and by God, he had been fortunate to run into them instead of Federal soldiers or road agents or outlaws. And more comforting, and oddly warming, was the information that the blue-eyed beauty was the same age as he was. And also an orphan. It was strange how intimately *nice* that was—not to be an orphan, certainly, but to share the same sort of life with a woman he had never known until now. But how could he tell them about John Brown and his part in the raid on Harpers Ferry—Good God!—Harpers Ferry. It came to him like a thunderbolt in the midst of his lulling sense of false security and delicious healing of his body. Had the raid come off? Had the old man been successful? Was the whole country aware of the raid?

"We're waiting, son. Tell us about yourself. In your own words. Take your time." Martinius Rheinbeck's dark brown eyes leveled at him. "We will listen and we will understand. There is nothing so bad that we cannot hear it from your own lips."

David Bard swallowed, nodding. And opened his mouth to speak.

He was amazed at himself, for the lies came so easily, the fabrications so swiftly, as though he had planned the story all along. To explain to this strange man and his strange companion who and what he was—knowing somehow that they would believe anything he told them.

"My name is Bard—David Bard."

"A good name. David means *beloved*. Go on."

"I'm nineteen, too. My folks both died on me years ago. Pa was killed by a drunken soldier from Fort Necessity, and Ma—well, she died giving birth—and me, well, I've been on my own ever since. Sold our farm in East Brunswick and moved out to Ohio. Then Virginia, working any kind of job I could. And you see, well, I was raised a Catholic and I do believe in the Almighty and I got no argument with those that think different. I do cotton to freedom. Of all kinds. I got no use for slavery, same as you folks and—'' He halted and Martinius Rheinbeck stared at him meaningfully. Edna Sunset had turned just once, to fling a quick look at him. He saw by her compassionate eyes that his being an orphan had registered on her. Then she turned away again, just as quickly. The wagon had topped the grade and was now lumbering down a gradually dipped trail. Tree-filled forests surrounded them on all sides. The wind was picking up too, building into a strong breeze. Edna Sunset's gloriously long blonde hair was bobbing to and fro. David pulled his eyes away from her, back to the bearded giant before him. He was not out of the woods yet.

"Go on, David." It was almost a command, as soft as it was.

And then the real lie came. The great lie. With mounting enthusiasm and a personal engrossment in his own tall story, David recounted an adventure, or misadventure, that might have come out of a book he had read. How upon finishing a day's work about two miles south of Harpers Ferry, clearing rocks for a farmer named Tolliver, he had been on his way back to his room and board in the widow Adams' house when he had been fallen upon by two strangers. Who had beaten him, stolen his wages, stripped his pockets, and left him for dead in the woods. He had come to much later and started off with no sense of direction because he was bleeding so badly and was half out of his head when he had come upon the Conestoga and the preacher and his companion. The rest he did not know. Could not know—hadn't he been delirious?

"How long have I been in this wagon, anyways?"

"You came to us yesterday before sundown. You have slept around the clock since then. Sister Edna washed your face and tended to your cuts and bruises. I bandaged your shoulder. Fortunately for you, the ball passed on through and I did not have to dig for the lead."

David blinked again.

"All that time? I musta been a drag on you—"

"You are one of the children of God. We are his servants. It was our duty. Say no more about it. You will make proper recompense when the time is right. It is enough for us that you will get well."

"I'm much obliged to you, Mr. Rheinbeck."

"You will call me Martinius as Sister Edna does. I insist on that. I am Mister to no man on this earth."

The word *recompense* bothered David Bard, but he kept his tongue still. It was enough that he was safe, with a good chance of mending properly and getting back on his feet again. But Martinius Rheinbeck was not done with him yet. Suddenly he reached under his black frock coat and produced something in the sunlight of the interior of the wagon. David's blood ran cold.

It was the Bowie knife. The drunken corporal's ugly weapon. With its horn handle and long, curved, single-edged blade. The thing had been cleaned, obviously, for it shone like a star now. Martinius Rheinbeck held it aloft, pointing the tip of the blade to the roof of the wagon. "David?" The preacher murmured his name gently.

"Yes, Martinius . . ."

"You came to us out of the forest, half dead, out on your feet, yet you were still clutching this in your right hand. Do you remember that at all?"

David shook his head dumbly, unready with a lie. For he did not remember, truly. The entire fight was a distorted memory, fading.

"This is a Bowie knife," Martinius Rheinbeck intoned. "Used for skinning deer and, alas, for fighting. Designed by the man who fell at the Alamo, James Bowie. A bad and notorious weapon on all counts, though Bowie was a good man. A Christian man. Tell me true, David Bard, did you kill a man with this knife?"

"God help me, Martinius . . ." David blurted, and paused.

"Yes, David?"

"I did not. I didn't—"

"Good. I am glad. It is enough for me that you have said so." Martinius Rheinbeck plunged the Bowie into the wooden floor of the wagon. "We will, however, keep the weapon. The 'Arkansas toothpick' can be of use to us. A weapon is only as good as the man who uses it, my son." David watched, almost in fascination, as the knife quivered and then was still, settled into the floor like an arrow. Martinius Rheinbeck stirred and reached into the frock coat once more, unearthing a round timepiece whose lid he clicked open with a snap of sound. The watch was carried on a heavy gold-linked chain which rode in one vest pocket attached to a leather fob.

"Sister Edna," Martinius Rheinbeck called, "it is high time we nooned. Pull off the road. I think also our David Bard would not be saying nay to a mess of corn fritters and some good hot coffee. It appears to me that I am hungry, too.''

''Yes, Martinius,'' Sister Edna replied in her soft, melodious voice and drew rein, pulling expertly on the leather ribbons in her hand. The Conestoga slowed; the horses stilled, gratefully. For the sun was now beating down unmercifully despite the lateness of the fall season. It was uncommonly warm for October, although Indian summer was in full swing. The last harvest was going on now all over the land before the killing chill and frost of the coming winter.

David Bard stared up at the canvas roof of the Conestoga.

His brain was flying, his mind a seething field of doubts, worries, and confusions. Yes, he was safe for now, with these two good people. But what of tomorrow and the tomorrow after that and the very future itself. How was he to get back to John Brown and the others? What did they think of him? Did they think he had deserted? Run off at the first sound of gunfire? Turned tail like a frightened chicken and run from the enemy? He didn't know.

The not-knowing made him very upset and uncomfortable. So much so that all his aches and pains had gone. He almost wanted to get up and run now. To get back to John Brown. Where he belonged. With all the others at Harpers Ferry. Fighting against slavery.

''David?'' Martinius Rheinbeck spoke from the depths of the driver's platform as Edna Sunset had dismounted on some errand when they had come to a full stop off the roadway under the shelter of a grove of juniper trees. A fine smell of forest and evergreen filled the air. Some dogwood trees sprouted off to the left, a small circle of beauty forever. The breezes wafted over wagon and horses.

"Yes, Martinius?"

"Did you honor your father and your mother?"

David Bard smiled. "I sure did. Pa would have laid me out if I didn't—but they were good to me—real good— they always were and I knew where I was with them. A son can't ask for more than that."

"Did you love them?"

"I did—more now than ever—why is it we always know something for a fact when it's kinda too late to do anything about it?"

Martinius Rheinbeck's answering smile was so warm and gentle that David knew that the bearded giant had thoroughly approved of all of his answers. The hawk nose seemed to wag, satisfied.

"It is the way of the Lord to test us, David Bard. So that we will be worthy when we enter the Gates of Heaven. Think of it in that way and your mind will be at peace."

"If you say so, Martinius—"

"I do say so, David."

"Fair enough, but it strikes me that's a pretty sad way to test a body's faith—killing off his father and mother."

Edna Sunset suddenly loomed in the circular opening at the rear of the wagon. Her beautiful face seemed framed in a painting. David gazed upon her, thinking to himself what a pleasure it might always be to look upon the face of Edna Sunset.

"You stay put, David Bard. We'll see to your needs. Take a few minutes to cook things up. But I'll bring you some coffee right off—it will be black, but it will be good. Milk and sugar we haven't got—all right with you?"

"That's just fine, Sister Edna." He was still marveling at her when the question popped out of him before he even considered the propriety of asking such a thing. "Is Sunset your real name, sure enough? I mean it's a peculiar name for a woman to have."

Edna Sunset's exquisite face clouded ever so slightly. The blue eyes saddened once more. The Cupid's-bow mouth quivered gently.

"The sun was going down over Lake Otsego when I was born in Cooperstown. My mother called me that all the time—I don't carry my family name anymore. . . . I don't want to remember all the bad in my life. I'm for Good now. Always. With Martinius Rheinbeck. The Good Lord cleared my head so that I don't hate Indians anymore for butchering my folks—I don't hate anybody. . . ." She hesitated, then almost flushed, shaking herself. "I'll get you some coffee now."

With that she was gone again, like some spirit in a dream.

David Bard settled back on his sick man's pallet.

There was an awful lot to think about once more.

Too much maybe for a man who never had finished his schooling. And book learning. Too complex, perhaps, for a young fellow who had known nothing but hard times and lovelessness these past several years. David groaned inwardly and idly roved a hand over his still tender face. He winced where he touched lacerations and bruises.

From outside, he could hear Edna Sunset humming again.

It was not "Rock of Ages" this time. Not by a jugful.

It was something else. Another hymn that David Bard also knew. One that was fast becoming as popular and well-known as "Rock of Ages" Yes, "Nearer My God to

Thee'' . . . that was what Edna Sunset was humming as she went about readying the noon meal.

What were the words again? How did the thing go?

Nearer, my God, to Thee,
 Nearer to Thee!
E'en though it be a Cross
 That raiseth me;
Still all my song shall be,
 Nearer, my God, to . . .

David Bard frowned, forgetting the hymn and the humming voice.

He had to wonder, truly wonder, just how much of his story and explanation for his battered condition that Martinius Rheinbeck truly believed. The bearded preacher might be a religious nut, a Holy Joe, but he was nobody's fool. That was pretty obvious, right enough.

David had had enough religious upbringing himself not to laugh at any man who believed in the Bible. The Good Book.

But he also did not know that the local militia at Harpers Ferry had rallied and had cut off any escape of John Brown and his men from the captured arsenal. Bottled up within the confines of the place he had wanted so desperately to seize and successfully loot, the Ohio farmer was poised for the final step in his mad deed. With his dead and dying comrades all about him. Old Osawatomie maintained a steady defense of his position, but the cards were stacked against him. Hard-riding Colonel Robert E. Lee and the platoon of cavalryman were already bearing down upon the fort. There was a reckoning coming, and John Brown would have to pay the piper. Dearly.

Even as Colonel Lee and his troopers rode, Martinius

Rheinbeck, Edna Sunset, and David Bard shared their first meal together in the bright sunlight along the trail to Kentucky. Under a sea-blue sky.

Beans, corn fritters, black bread, and lots of coffee.

Barrels filled with fresh creek water hung lashed to the sides of the Conestoga wagon, as well as digging implements, a huge axe, a two-handed saw, and canvas bags holding hardtack and jerky, the dried-meat of the plains that would keep in all climates without the need of freezing. A buffalo hide hung suspended from the rear of the wagon. Martinius Rheinbeck used this as a robe in cold weather, his one concession to a luxury along the trail—a robe he shared with Edna Sunset when they rode together up front behind the horses.

The frying pan and coffeepot had been stored in the box under the driver's seat. Those and tin cups with handles on them. All in all, Martinius Rheinbeck had set up a fine rig. Trail life was never easy, but at least the preacher had started out well.

And then there was that large, unmarked, nailed-tight wooden crate lying alongside the opposite end of the Conestoga. David Bard wondered about that, too.

He did not have to wonder long.

"Bibles, David. A full one hundred copies of the Good Book," Martinius Rheinbeck nearly exulted, as he spooned a mouthful of beans into the center of the triangular black beard. "Bought them for next to nothing from a foolish nonbeliever selling books in the streets of Roanoke—I will need them for our work in Horsefall. It was a bargain all in all—those boooks will spread the word throughout the land. More beans or fritters, son?"

"Thank you—no. I've eaten enough so that I'm fit to

bust. Sister Edna cooks real good. Those fritters were powerful tasty.''

''Amen to that, boy. Most times she whips them up with some fruit in them, but this is not the season for them, I fear.''

David could not see where Edna Sunset was, having her own meal, but he sensed her presence nearby as surely as he saw Martinius Rheinbeck squatted on the riding platform of the wagon. The woman had an aura, a special something, which he would not have been able to put into the proper words. Martinius Rheinbeck would know the words and how to use them. But David Bard did not.

Still, as good as all this was, the friendly preacher and his angel, the comfort of the wagon and the food, he could not take his thoughts away from yesterday. And the raid and how it had all begun and that crazy soldier—with a sudden jolt he realized something. Something that had not struck him until this very moment.

Pa had been killed by a drunken man in the blue uniform of the United States Army. And yesterday the very same thing had almost happened to him. The son of that man. Like father, like son.

''*Judas Iscariot!*'' Martin Rheinbeck suddenly thundered, poking his spoon skyward. ''Look up there—I declare—the sky is full of vultures! *Thunderation!* I smell Evil.''

And so the sky was—literally alive with the ugly black birds.

Martin Rheinbeck's nose did not deceive him, either.

The bawling screech of the baldheaded, hook-beaked flying parasites of the heavens was far too close not to be taken seriously.

Something was in the wind. Something ugly and fearful.

Death was nearby.

Where there were buzzards, there was always death.

"We best be hitching up the horses again," Martinius Rheinbeck declared solemnly. "Those birds are an omen from the Lord. A sign that godlessness is near. Sister Edna, let us move on. David will remain in the wagon where he will be safe. It is too soon to ask him to do a man's work again."

David Bard did not protest.

Temporarily, in his weakened condition, there was little fight left in him. Though the shotguns were near at hand and he could use those if need be. As well as the Bowie knife still poking upward from the wooden floor of the Conestoga wagon.

The Bowie knife with which he had killed a man.

And lied to another man about. Bald-facedly.

A man of God, to boot.

David Bard restrained a shudder for his immortal soul.

THREE GODLESS MEN

The trail had become more difficult, the worn roadway soon turning to grass and rock, as if the old byway had ended somewhere all too subtly. The four horses were hard put to draw the huge wagon and its load of three people and so many supplies carefully and comfortably. The wagon shifted, swayed, and bounced. David clung to his cot, trying to steady himself. The wooden crate and the grain bags moved about, crowding him. Martinius Rheinbeck used his strong hands on the reins as Sister Edna Sunset held fast to her seat at his side. And still, up above, the flight of ugly vultures seemed to keep pace with them, even if it was only an illusion. It had been some twenty minutes since they had quit their campsite, but now it looked as if the bearded Rheinbeck was drawing closer to the buzzards overhead rather than away from them.

Edna Sunset, hand placed to her forehead, for she wore

no bonnet, peered up at them, against the bright glare of sunlight.

"Why do they circle like that, Martinius? What are they waiting for?"

"Some poor creature is dying on the ground. They can smell death for it is a meal for them. Let us hope the creature is a four-legged one close to the end of its mortal misery."

"And if it is a two-legged one?"

Martinius Rheinbeck shrugged his broad shoulders.

"Then he or she should die with a few good words spoken over them before they meet their Maker, Sister."

"It's awful, just the same, Martinius. To be eaten by filthy birds such as those."

"Amen to that, Sister. But it is the way of life."

While this exchange was passing between the preacher and the woman, David Bard had raised himself to a sitting position so that he could see better. Past their forms, which blocked the opening of the wagon, he got a cramped view of the roadway and the horizon. But all he saw was a wilderness of trees now. The terrain, save for the gentle rises of the roadway, was flatter than a pancake.

"There!" Martinius Rheinbeck suddenly shouted. "Look you, Sister. They're coming down—all of them—"

"Can't be more than a quarter of a mile away," she murmured in answer, awe still in her musical voice. "I don't want to see it."

"No need for that. The location is off-trail. We will not pass by. But I will say a prayer to myself if it should be some poor mortal dying out yonder."

"Then I will too, Brother Martinius."

They bowed their heads before him, and he marveled

once again at their mutual understanding of each other. But the part of him that was young flesh and blood somehow found their Christianity and soft-spoken words hypocritical and not very practical. This was a big country, and a rough one, and action was more to the point, not prayers and platitudes and homilies about the goodness of man and God. David Bard controlled a rising stab of anger and resentment. Those ugly vultures were sitting down to a meal, and that was all there was to that. Dog eat dog. Survival of the fittest. Hadn't John Brown told him that just last month, quoting from some book by an English fellow named Darwin, who showed that the world belonged to those that were strong enough to live in it?

Damn, but he had. . . .

All instinctively, David Bard reached out for one of the two shotguns lying on the floor of the covered wagon. He could not have said why, but never in his lifetime, this or any other, would he make a more timely gesture.

For suddenly, with a crashing halt and a rattle and jounce of all that the wagon held, Martinius Rheinbeck jerked savagely on the reins and the Conestoga lurched to a grinding stop. David felt himself flung from his cot even as his fingers closed over the stock of the weapon. And a strident, raucous, jeering male voice broke the stillness of the afternoon air: "HOLD ON THERE, GRANDPA! JUST SET STILL AND NOTHIN'S GOIN' TO HAPPEN. WILL! TOM! SEE THOSE HORSES DON'T SPOOK."

Holding his breath, lifting the shotgun gently, David Bard crawled to the wagon-side and peered under a buckle in the spread of canvas. There was merely a slit, but it gave him a ringside seat to all that was happening and had happened in the last few seconds. Martinius Rheinbeck had risen to his feet, arms folded in contempt, and Sister Edna remained where she was, her hands placed fearfully to the older man's side. And David Bard, not looking at them now, saw what had occurred through his canvas peephole.

There were three men coming down from a hillock of earth to the left of the Conestoga, stepping in plain view from a hiding place which had obviously concealed them from Martinius Rheinbeck's eyes until they sprang out and got the drop on him. Each of the men bore handguns, all of them trained on the driver's seat of the wagon where Martinius and the woman were stationed. Never had David Bard seen a more villainous-looking trio of bandits. For that is what they had to be. Road bandits, those predators of the trail. Living off the innocent horsemen and settlers in wagons who came their way.

These three were dressed in no particular uniformity of garb. Chances were very good that all that they wore were the spoils of their depredations along the trail. One wore a straw hat, another a Mexican sombrero, the third a foraging cap, U.S. Army issue. Their trousers were worn and faded, tucked into teamster's boots, and all of their shirts and bandanas were dirty and faded. David would never forget their faces, either. Grimy, unshaven, leering, with bad teeth showing from each coarse mouth. Even their weapons were varied and irregular. A horse pistol, a Derringer, and a Colt Navy revolver. But the trio had one thing, one feature, solidly in common. They were all mean and ugly and utterly without scruples.

"What do you want of us, Brothers?" Martinius Rheinbeck demanded. "If you seek food and water, we will share them with you. Of gold and riches, we have nothing.''

The leader of the three, barely inches taller than his companions, took a step forward, wagging the Navy revolver almost carelessly, obviously deciding for himself that this man and this woman were going to be no trouble at all. His guffaw of laughter blasted the stillness of the setting.

''Well, I'll be hornswoggled. You hear that, Will? You, Tom? We got ourselves one of them preacher-fellows and his woman. Daughter, maybe. Either way, he calls us brothers. He got that right, didn't he, brothers?''

''I do not understand you,'' Martinius Rheinbeck said sternly. ''Do not bar our way and let us pass in peace. We mean you no harm.''

Now all three really laughed, in unison, like three braying jackasses. David Bard quietly lifted the shotgun in the gloomy interior of the wagon and waited. The leader of the group—it was he who wore the foraging cap—suddenly stopped laughing and placed the Navy revolver against his right shoulder, as if it were too heavy.

''You the one who don't understand, mister. We be the Tarzy brothers. That's Will and Tom, and I be Pete. And we're gonna take your rig and all that's in it, especially that there girl, and then we're gonna leave you for the buzzards. The same ones that's feastin' on our dead horses back there. Damn critters drunk from a foul water hole afore we did. Lucky for us. Not so lucky for them.''

Martinius Rheinbeck dismounted from the wagon, placing his tall, broad-shouldered figure between the Tarzy brothers and Edna Sunset. He held out his long arms in supplication.

"Aye, you are sinners, all three of you. And you would sin again with what is mine. But I will not let you. Think and believe. The Lord is my companion. He goes with me. You cannot win against the Lord. Throw down your arms and pray with me, and I will be your salvation this day. Turn from the path of Evil to Righteousness, and the Lord will welcome you with open arms."

"Shoot him now, Pete," Will Tarzy, the sombrero-hatted Tarzy whined in a nasal voice. "Ah cain't stand preachers nohow."

"If you don't, Ah will," Tom Tarzy chortled, aiming the Derringer from a distance of three feet. "Always did want to see what one of these over-and-unders would do to a man's face at this range." The small pistol was a double-barreled 'sneak's weapon.'

Edna Sunset suddenly stirred from her frozen position on the wagon seat. "Your clothes are dirty, your faces are dirty, and your souls are dirty. But listen to Brother Martinius—he will help you. It's not too late to find the God that is in you all."

Pete Tarzy squinted at her in the sunlight and ran a wet tongue over his lower lip. His beady eyes glittered, taking in the full-figured, full-bosomed incomparable beauty of her. Abruptly, he chuckled low in his throat, pointed the Navy revolver at Martinius Rheinbeck, and said in a low voice: "There's enough of her for all three of us, brothers, but I get her first—after a few days, mebbe, you can have her." He cocked the hammer of the weapon and the sharp click of sound was as loud as any pistol shot.

Martinius Rheinbeck swore a mighty oath. But he was not afraid. He began a giant step forward, raising up one long arm to bring down upon Pete Tarzy's vicious face.

The other two brothers hooted and shouted with laughter, and even Pete Tarzy had to pause and fade back to get a second look at this crazy old man who stepped into the barrel of a gun without flinching. Or turning yellow.

David Bard could wait no longer. The moment was at hand.

The twin-barreled nose of the shotgun was already set on the lip of the wooden wagon-side where it met the lashed-down canvas covering. The Tarzy Brothers were all in his sights, lined up like three turkeys at a shooting match.

Martinius Rheinbeck's mighty arm cut a swath through empty air and Edna Sunset's voice rose in a shrill scream. Pete Tarzy, a wolfish grin showing yellow, crooked teeth, took dead aim at the older man's bearded face. There was no mistaking the ugly intent in that grin or the animallike gleam in those beady eyes.

David Bard triggered the shotgun. Later, much later, he realized it was one of the most simple and pleasurable things he had ever done. Without a moment's hesitation or even a mild consideration that he was killing another man. It wasn't at all like his hand-to-hand struggle with the drunken corporal. The Tarzy brothers were scum, the dregs of humanity, and dying was too good for any of them. Also, his feelings for Martinius Rheinbeck and Edna Sunset had already gone far beyond those that one might feel for mere acquaintances. It was also a question of property. The Tarzys had no rights to the Conestoga wagon. Or to anything and anyone that were a part of it. So David Bard fired with great pleasure and a greater satisfaction. Not even the Lord would have turned the other cheek to Pete, Will, and Tom Tarzy. No way in hell.

The thunder and roar of the shotgun blast rolled around
the clearing with great gobbling echoes. And Pete Tarzy
was blown clear backwards, head over heels, his arms
outflung in great surprise and amazement. He went down
and stayed down, and Will and Tom Tarzy stood like
statues for a full instant, their eyes flying open in shock
and terror. As if lightning had come down from the skies
above, indeed, the hand of God responding to the call of
the tall, black-suited giant before them. But the moment
did not last. They were ruffians and blackguards of the
lowest and highest order. Accustomed to in-fighting and
the dirty rules of gunplay. The burst of smoke from the
wagon now told them where the blast had come from.
They reacted much more quickly this time. Will Tarzy
threw himself to the ground, the sombrero riding to the
earth with him, dangling on its leather string past his
shoulders. His horse pistol came up and he blazed away.
His brother Tom lost his straw hat, too, as he fanned to the
other side of Pete Tarzy's dead, inert form. Edna Sunset
screamed something again, and Martinius Rheinbeck, without changing his positon, turned in amazement to stare
incredulously at the Conestoga wagon and the shotgun
barrels thrusting into plain sight. He was barely out of the
line of fire, but David Bard had no time to think about
that. Will Tarzy's shot had chewed a fistful of wood from
the wagon-side close to his face. Almost gleefully, David
tugged the second trigger of the shotgun.

Will Tarzy took the second load full in the face. His
features disappeared in a carmine burst of exploding flesh.
Long before his already dead corpse slumped to the green
earth, Tom Tarzy had taken the easy road to safety. Not
knowing just how many guns were ready to kill him from

the concealment of the Conestoga, and only having the dainty Derringer, that hideaway arm so favored by riverboat gamblers, Gold Rush dandies, and Western gunfighters because it was so easy to conceal—and seeing his two brothers blasted into oblivion right before his eyes—Tom Tarzy turned tail and ran. For cover and for his life. He took off like a crazed chicken with its head cut off and crashed out of the clearing, hurtling through the tall trees without looking back. The straw hat lay where he had left it. Between the silent, bloody corpses of Pete and Will Tarzy.

A great, almost awesome silence now closed over the clearing. David sagged back to his pallet, releasing the shotgun whose hot barrels now seemed to burn him. He was spent once more. Exhausted. As if the simple tugging of triggers had overtaxed him. But he knew better than that. He had killed his second and third man. All within the space of two days—he, David Bard, who had never so much as swung a fist in anger. His heart beat loudly. Amazingly, he was not contrite or feeling guilty. Killing the Tarzys was like catching up with the work he had missed at Harpers Ferry.

They were staring at him from the high seat of the wagon—not sitting, but flanking the platform, peering in at him where he lay. He would never forget the expressions on their faces. Martinius Rheinbeck's fierce, bearded visage was stern. The dark brown eyes were pinpointed with wonder and outrage. Sister Edna Sunset's smooth-curved countenance was drained of all color. The cornflower-blue eyes were looking at him as if truly seeing him for the very first time. For a long moment no one spoke. Then

Martinius Rheinbeck thundered in a voice that would have moved mountains.

"You had no call to do that! Killing them—their souls could have been saved."

"That's fool-talk, Martinius, and you know it. They were settin' to kill you. Good thing that shotgun was handy."

"He that lives by the sword shall die by the sword!" The preacher's voice rose on a note of further anger and rebuke.

David's gorge rose hotly.

"Don't talk like a damn—" He broke off, checking his own rage. Instead of getting thanks for saving all their necks, he was being scolded like any schoolboy! But he could see the hurt in their faces, especially Edna Sunset's. So he answered more gently than he wanted to. "Martinius, those fellows were no more'n a step from blowing your head off. You heard them. What they were fixin' to do with Edna—you think I was going to stand by—"

"You could have told them to throw down their weapons, David," Martinius Rheinbeck said sadly. His vocal thunder had lowered.

"Fellows like that? Not a chance. There was a rope waiting for them all their lives. Somewhere. No, I tell you. It wouldn't have done any good. Besides, there was no time—he already was squeezing the trigger on you when I fired."

"Thou shalt not kill, David."

"Better they kill us, Martinius? All of us? If that's what you call turning the other cheek I want no part of it."

Martinius Rheinbeck shook himself. The almost insane look of religious zeal left his eyes. His face softened.

"I suppose you are right. You have saved our lives. I

only wish you had not had to kill to do that. We thank you, Sister Edna and I. We owe you much.''

"You don't owe me anything. It was my neck as well as yours if the Tarzys had their way with us.''

"I am thanking you, too, David,'' Edna Sunset barely breathed the words. "God's will be done.'' Her golden hair glowed in the sun.

"You're more than welcome, Edna. And don't you be worrying about the other fellow. He won't be back. He'll want no part of this outfit, the way I see it. He's gone for good.''

The preacher nodded, mutely agreeing. He tugged his hat-brim.

"We will give the brothers a Christian burial. They were sinners, but they were men in God's image . . .''

"God better not look like them,'' David said firmly. "Or I'm not so sure I'd cotton to ever meeting him.''

"Don't be profane, son. They were born same as you and I. And they lost their way. No one is whelped bad. The evils of this life of ours do things to men. You're still young—you will learn.''

"All right. I will. If you say so.'' David Bard smiled thinly. "But don't ask me to help you bury them. I wouldn't touch vermin like them with a ten-foot pole.''

"Very well. It shall be as you say. I do not wish you to exert yourself, as it is. There will be work for you to do later. But not now. Sister Edna will assist me.''

"Don't ask her to do that—'' David began to protest.

But Sister Edna Sunset cut into his words with a beatific smile and a steady voice that held no fear or disgust.

"Don't mind, David. I do not. It's god's work, and I am his servant, too. I'll get the shovels, Martinius.''

David Bard shook his head in wonder.

"If it was up to me, I'd be leaving their carcasses for those same buzzards that ate their poor horses."

"It is not up to you, David Bard," Martinius Rheinbeck intoned, without rancor. "It is up to me. I am the shepherd here. I will tend my flock."

There was no more to be said.

David rolled over on his pallet and closed his eyes against the glare of sunlight. He was tired once more. A great weariness was stealing over him, though there was much to think about and ponder over. These strange people, always talking about God and acting as if varmints and skunks like the Tarzy brothers were real people and not lowlifes—they had meant to shoot Martinius Rheinbeck and then pleasure themselves with Sister Edna: The mere thought of that made David's blood boil. How in tarnation could Martinius Rheinbeck call such scum Christians? It was beyond him. . . .

Within the hour the two Tarzy brothers lay under the earth. Martinius Rheinbeck had dug down only far enough to cover them. Two small wooden crosses, fashioned by Sister Edna from twigs and leather thongs to brace them, marked the gravesites in the clearing. Unmarked graves, but Christian graves all the same. David watched from the peephole in the wagon-side. The tall, bearded giant of a preacher-man, read aloud from the Bible when the bodies were down under. The Twenty-Third Psalm. How many times in the past had he heard Ma and Pa speak that one: *"The Lord is my shepherd; I shall not want. He maketh me to lie down in green pastures . . ."*

Rheinbeck's voice rose in the wilderness, building in the power of his resonance and clarity. David hardly listened.

He could not take his eyes away from Edna Sunset. She was in profile to him, and now he could really see the slender shapeliness of her, the full upthrust of her bosom in the gingham dress, so female, so womanly. Her exquisite face with the marvelous nose and mouth and that long, flowing golden-corn hair—when he thought of what the Tarzys had intended for her, a hot flash stirred his own vitals. A long dormant desire stabbed at him, meaningfully. He had not had many women. Not but two that he could remember. Effie Slagg back there in East Brunswick on that hayride in from the school picnic. He'd been no more than a tad then. And then, years later, when he was seventeen, that bawdy house woman in New Brunswick when he had gone to see about a load of bricks because Mr. Ellis wanted to build a new well behind his farmhouse—Aurelie, her name was. You couldn't forget a name like that. And she had been French and almost old enough to be his mother, but she had taught him things about his body and his male desires that he had never known. Or experienced. Yes, Aurelie. Her bedroom, *boudoir* she called it, had been all of a boy's wildest fancies come true. . . .

"Ah, David, *pauvre garçon* . . . you want Aurelie, eh?"

"M'am?"

"Then you shall have me . . . there . . . my legs are parted. . . ."

The sudden memory was pulsing, pounding.

But now, Sister Edna Sunset—Lord, but she was prime. . . .

David cursed under his breath, all too conscious of the rude awakening of his manhood below the belt buckle. He turned away from the burial services scene and closed his eyes tightly, pulling the woolen blankets up over his head. Still, Martinius Rheinbeck's inescapable voice reached him through the walls of the wagon.

". . . .*He restoreth my soul: He leadeth me in the paths of* . . .''

He turned his thoughts to John Brown again. Almost as a refuge from the preacher-man. Harpers Ferry still nettled him. He wished he knew if the surprise raid had been successful. And what had the U.S. government done about it? If anything. But they had to have done something, hadn't they? After all, they just couldn't let a man take over one of their important arsenals without getting plenty riled up.

"*. . . Yea, though I walk through the valley of the shadow . . . I will fear no evil. . . .*''

Martinius Rheinbeck's powerful voice was lulling him. Just like Ma reading him to sleep back there in New Jersey—he might have been a child once more, listening to a loving parent.

He had fallen asleep before the preacher finished the psalm and he and Sister Edna Sunset had returned to the wagon. Not even Rheinbeck's command to the waiting horses or the shifting of the iron wheels into sudden motion stirred him. His riotous mind, feverish with a dozen diverse, confusing, conflicting thoughts, had given away to slumber. Again, a peaceful one. His young muscles relaxed, spread out, and surrendered to the great weariness that had stolen over him since the morning. Killing will do that to a man, too. As soldiers coming off combat had always learned to their great surprise. The body and the soul and the mind does not take to killing, any kind of killing, and needs restoring.

The Conestoga moved out, cresting the gradual slope of the nearest hill, clattering past the hillocks, trees, and boulders as Martinius Rheinbeck found the trail toward Kentucky. And Horsefall. Past Gate City below the Cumberland Valley.

The ugly baldheaded buzzards could no longer be seen in the overhead sky. There was nothing but azure blue vastness with white clouds so motionless the heavens might have been a painting in oils. The pale sun was dipping to the horizon, blazing with less fire and heat. The winds had quickened anew. The Shenandoah Mountains rose grandly off to the north. Martinius Rheinbeck knew his route from long porings over the maps of the land. He drove the horses and the wagon due west. Into the setting sun. Where his own flock waited. For a holy man to bring them the Good Word from the Good Book.

David Bard slept as the Conestoga lumbered on, rocking, swaying, wheels turning. Churning westward.

Hardly knowing that before him lay the Great Adventure.

And a life he had never bargained for. Or dreamed about.

Or thought possible or likely.

With a man and a woman he had only met yesterday.

John Brown, his long, flowing white beard flecked with blood, stared forlornly through the stone-bounded window nearest at hand at Harpers Ferry. His glazed eyes spoke volumes for the situation he now found himself and his followers in. The arsenal had been taken with barely a struggle, but holding it had been another matter entirely. A horse of a far different color. For hours on end the Harpers Ferry militia below the stone face of the arsenal had placed the Brown party under siege with constant firing and a never-ending pounding of small cannon. The arsenal was a shambles now. What was the use of capturing all these guns and ammunition if he could not escape with them and his men to the protection of the mountains where he could truly fight his fight against slavery?

All about him the wounded and the dying added their woeful chorus of moans to his gloomy thoughts. Two of his boys were already dead. Killed in the first retaliatory fusillade of the militia of the town. And surely, the Government itself would be sending reinforcements soon—to make him pay for his act of sedition. Yes, he had overplayed his hand. Never thinking that the pitifully small local militia at Harpers Ferry could have blocked him in such a forceful manner. The Ohio farmer turned from the window, his peculiar short sword stained with blood and dust, dragging in his tired right hand. Within him the drums of defeat sounded.

Lord, Lord, help me, Thy servant, in my hour of need.

As if in mocking answer to his silent prayer, the frenzied shout of his remaining sun, Caleb, split the choking, powder-scented atmosphere of the low-ceilinged arsenal:

"PAW! LOOK! THERE'S A WHOLE TROOP OF U.S. CAVALRY COMIN'—THAT DOES IT FOR US, DON'T IT, PAW?"

John Brown shook himself, closing his eyes, stiffening his back. Once more he strode to the designated window where Caleb Brown was pointing excitedly. The wounded and the dying whimpered aloud. The lanky, white-bearded Brown joined Caleb at the window. He stared out into the hard daylight. What he saw made his soul shrivel and die. Caleb had seen true: They were finished—all of them.

Beyond the square fronting the arsenal proper, at furious gallop, came a troop of cavalrymen, plumes flying, sabers gleaming in the sun, rifles at the ready. Before them charged a handsome officer on horseback. The epitome of the U.S. cavalryman. A bugle pierced the air, sending a strident battle cry to the heavens.

John Brown raised his sword. His eyes gleamed starkly.

"To the windows, all of you! Hold your fire until I give the command. By the Eternal, we will make them pay with blood if they think to take us without a fight. Remember, this is the Lord's battle and we are His soldiers. Right is on our side. . . ."

There was a mad scramble for the windows, the remainder of the eighteen men he had brought with him into the arsenal, clawing for a good gun position. John Brown had long since forgotten about one of his lost sheep—David Bard. Who might be lying dead out there, even now, another fallen angel in God's holy crusade.

John Brown raised the short broadsword.

His eyes were like hollows of madness now.

Down below, out there, Colonel Robert E. Lee, wheeling his platoon to a graceful halt, called for Split Ranks in a clear, crisp voice so that one half of his command veered to the left and the other half to the right. It was a very graceful military maneuver. His junior officers, Custer and Stuart, knew what they were about. The troopers moved smartly, efficiently.

The Harpers Ferry situation was now officially in hand.

The United States Government had answered John Brown's challenge. With an armed force, ready to make him pay for his insurrection against country and flag.

"FIRE AT WILL!" Old Osawatomie Brown thundered.

The air inside the arsenal came alive with rifle fire.

TRAIL PEOPLE

The sizzling sound and unmistakable aroma of bacon frying brought David Bard out of a deep sleep. Darkness greeted his eyes, and then the low glow of firelight showed him the stars and a full moon. He struggled erect, only then feeling a sharp twinge in the shoulder which had received the drunken corporal's crazed shot. The bandage, a crudely fashioned bit of white sheet and gauze now showed a dried stain. Still, he felt pretty fine generally. The many naps were doing him a lot of good. He wondered if he would be able to navigate. He decided to try. In the gloom of the wagon's interior he raised himself from the pallet and reached for the driver's platform, pulling himself forward. So far, so good. He heard no voices at all, but the sound of the frying bacon and the firelight was reassuring. The preacher and the woman must be up and about, preparing the evening meal. He was sure it was the same day, somehow, though he had no time-piece like Martinius Rheinbeck's.

He was right, for no sooner had he loomed from the wagon's interior than he heard Rheinbeck's now familiar voice call out: "It is well that you are awake, David. You need your rest, aye, but I think some nourishing food will do you much better."

"How are you feeling, David?" Edna Sunset's sweet voice came to him, as though in a dream.

He turned toward their voices. He could not have explained the sense of family, of belonging, that washed over him as he once again saw their unique faces and figures.

They were hunkering down around a small fire built of saplings and twigs. Martinius Rheinbeck had removed his black frock coat but not his hat. The sight of him in white-sleeved shirt was somehow reassuring. The preacher was holding a coffeepot above the flames, while Edna Sunset was gently shaking a huge frying pan in which strips of bacon crackled and curled. She had rolled up the sleeves of her gingham dress and her arms gleamed smooth and golden in the firelight. David eased down stiffly from the wagon. It felt good to be on his feet again. But somehow he was all too conscious of his worn pants, scuffed boots, and dirty shirt. His face still flamed from all the cuts and bruises, but that too was wearing off. In truth, he felt better with each passing second.

"That looks powerful good," he sighed, as Martinius Rheinbeck passed him a tin cup of scalding hot coffee. He took it, nodding his thanks. "I should have asked before but where have you both been sleeping?"

Martinius Rheinbeck shrugged his broad shoulders.

"Nothing lost, David. The weather has been God's own. Sister Edna and I have been taking our sleep around the campfire at night. The wagon is yours until you are well enough. And welcome to it."

"But it isn't fair—"

"Hush, David," Edna Sunset admonished him, smiling. "I like it outdoors. Truly. Until it rains or gets colder, you'll get no complaints from me."

He blew on the coffee, cooling it, then sipping, as his hands warmed around the hot tin. His eyes found hers, but she had turned away, lowering her attention to the frying bacon. So he looked at Martinius Rheinbeck instead. The older man was surveying him with odd purposefulness. "Something wrong, Martinius?"

"Nothing that I cannot cure. There is a cool lake close by. I made camp here intentionally. I would suggest after supper you divest yourself of those ill-used garments. I will burn them. In the wagon you will find a set of buckskins. Trousers, jacket, a hat to match. They are just about your size, my boy, and they are yours. I'm sorry I cannot provide fresh boots. Yours will have to do until we reach a town again. The water will be good for your wounds."

"That's mighty generous of you, Martinius."

"It is more blessed to give than to receive, David."

"Who'd the buckskins belong to?"

"They belong to my past, boy. That is all you need know. I am sure they will be a passable fit on you."

"Then I'm much obliged."

"Duly noted and understood. Now, we'll pass out the plates. This is no banquet, but coffee and bacon and bread will serve this cool October night—Sister Edna?"

When the food was ready and before they all dug in, the older man said grace in his usual, ministerial manner. Sister Edna and he lowered their heads. David Bard did not, watching them, and marveling once again at how fate had thrown him in with such a strange pair. It was difficult to say how old Martinius Rheinbeck might be. His face was bronzed and unlined and his beard was coal-black. But he had to be of middle age—or did he? As for Sister Edna, had she not admitted to nineteen years; he could have been forgiven for thinking she was in her twenties. Despite the obvious bloom of health and beauty in her face, there was something *older* about her. She had matured early. She carried herself with the dignity and style. Like a woman gentle born—like a lady in *Lady Godey's Book*.

The meal of bacon, bread, and hot black coffee was just right. And there was more than enough to go around, though he noted that the preacher and Sister Edna ate sparingly. So he did not make like a glutton. But he did finish off the coffee. It warmed him full down to his toes and he could feel his blood surge with fresh vitality.

The Conestoga with the unhitched horses stood against a protective bower of elm trees. The other side of the camp-site was flat, unbroken terrain plunging off into a wilderness of darkness. He could make out the dim outline of the mountain range far off in the distance. The full moon above provided almost enough light to read by.

"Which way is the lake, Martinius?"

"About fifty yards beyond those elms. I have already availed myself of its waters. It's plumb refreshing, son. You will feel like a new man once you have cleansed yourself."

"Anything might be an improvement, Martinius."

Even Rheinbeck recognized the jibe and smiled.

"Go, rascal, and sin no more. We will see to the supper plates and the fire."

"I'll do that, Martinius." He glanced at Sister Edna Sunset. "That was just fine, Edna. Thank you."

"You are welcome, David Bard."

Was he imagining things or was there something in her low tone, something more than courtesy and etiquette? He shook himself and stretched erect. It felt good to be alive. Out here with these two. Amazingly, he had not thought of John Brown once since he had awakened. And Sister Edna was talking to him again: "When you're done, I'll make a fresh bandage for your shoulder, if need be. You have to keep infection away."

"All right. I won't be too long."

"Take as long as you please, David. There's no telling when we'll reach fresh water again before Kentucky."

Nodding, he returned to the wagon and found the buckskin garments in a neat pile, with a handsome hat, too, atop the unmarked crate that held the Bibles. They looked right nice, and somehow he felt exhilarated. In his hands the buckskins were warm and pleasant to the touch. They would be delightful to don once he had rid himself of his grimy, worn clothes and taken that swim in the lake. Now he could hardly wait. He left the hat behind.

Humming to himself, he set out for the elms. Sister Edna and Rheinbeck were busy with the campfire, cleaning up a mite. David Bard was amazed to find himself humming under his breath. The night air was clear and cooling. He hadn't gone five yards but that he realized he was humming "Rock of Ages."

Repressing a short, hard laugh, he found the lake shining softly in the moonlight. The moon made silvery shafts of beauty upon its still waters. It looked plumb inviting, all right.

Still humming, David Bard undressed rapidly.

He spent a full half hour in the water, finding that unusual balm of soul and body that did not come often enough for those that lived in the early days of the country's growth. There never was enough time or opportunity for bathing. Water was precious, especially for drinking and survival. But this was paradise, indeed. So he rocked and reveled and plunged and made a great splashing tour of the lake. His body welcomed the change from grime and dirt and dust, not to mention the good being done for his cuts and bruises and the stiffening shoulder wound. For all of thirty minutes he swam, and then David Bard felt like a new man. He had always been able to swim since Pa taught him how to dog-paddle across Farrington Lake in New Jersey. He had been only abot seven then, and soon enough he was able to slice the lake with expert strokes so that his mother would often remark, "That boy is part catfish, Michael Winship Bard."

"That he be, Frances. That he be. . . ."

It didn't hurt to think of them like that after all this time of loss. But it made him thoughtful so that he quieted down in his heart and head and finished the swim in easy silence.

When he returned to the campsite, he was new-born.

His old garments were folded over his arm and the buckskin outfit fit him as well as if he had bought them at the general store. He and the preacher were of the same size. Six good feet of maleness, broad-shouldered into a compact one hundred and seventy-five pounds. It was Martinius Rheinbeck's *air* to seem taller.

David had not shaved, for his face still stung and the slight hair stubbling his chin and jaws could hold until he borrowed Martinius Rheinbeck's razor. His long, uncut dark brown hair clung uncombed to his head. But that did not matter, either. Never had he felt so alive, so young, so good—so right.

Sister Edna Sunset was waiting for him by the dying campfire. Off to the left, not far from the flames, Martinius Rheinbeck lay stretched out in a deep sleep. He did not snore. The great, bearded, hawk-nosed face was peaceful. The conical, wide-brimmed hat rested atop the woolen blanket drawn up to the preacher's throat. David Bard stared down at him for a moment, smiling, then joined Edna Sunset around the fire. She was squatting, her legs crossed Indian-style, regarding the last burning embers with such intent that he thought she might be divining them.

"Sister Edna?" he almost whispered, tentative.

Her face turned to him and she smiled. The cornflower-blue eyes were never lovelier, nor more mysterious.

"My, you look nice, David. They look well on you."

"We're both big sixes, I reckon."

"Martinius was tired. He said to say good night to you."

David shook his head. "He's some man, he is. Never did meet a one like him."

"He is a great man, David. One day everyone will know."

"But you know, don't you?"

"That I do."

"Then that's all that counts. In the long run."

There was a brief silence between them now. A silence that held a meaning he could not find. He studied her in the firelight. She took his breath away. And that was a fact. Those blue eyes, the long, golden hair—he was suddenly aware that the gingham dress was unbuttoned below her throat and the rising curve of her bosom was bared enough to make him feel dry in the mouth and uneasy all around. The blood was beginning to move in his veins. The hands which he had only recently washed seemed to tingle. He shook himself.

"Are you all right, David?" She was eyeing him closely.

"I'm fine," he lied.

"That shoulder looks pretty good now. No swelling. And the wound closed real good—maybe it would be best not to bandage it again. The fresh air would be a sight better for healing."

"I'll do anything you say, Edna. It doesn't hurt at all."

She smiled and the blue eyes lost their concern.

"Is there anything you want to tell me, David?"

"Meaning?"

"You told us what happened. I don't mean that. I mean before. Where you lived, what your folks were like—what you want to do with the rest of your days."

"Hold on, now." He laughed in spite of himself. "That's a tall order. Too much for one night. I'll say this, though, and tell you I'm glad I'm here. With you. And him." He jerked a shoulder at the sleeping giant. "I was a man going nowhere. Without any kind of direction. Right now I feel a whole lot better about things. Throwin' in with you and Martinius seems right fine to me."

"You're but nineteen," Sister Edna Sunset said calmly. "But you don't talk like a boy. You talk like a man."

"A boy grows up pretty fast when he loses his kinfolk before he's old enough to shave. You ought to know. You're an orphan, too, I recollect, and you don't sound like no kid, either. Not by a jugful. If I'd had to guess, I would have said you were a lot older than nineteen, too."

She lowered her eyes, almost shyly. He waited for her to speak again, trying to collect his own feelings which were building far too fast. He was conscious of everything about her, the merest look, the slightest gesture. He was man enough also to know that he was in trouble. He was hers anytime she asked him or indicated as much. He put his hands together in a clasp to steady them.

"David . . ."

"Yeah?" The moon and the stars never seemed brighter to him.

"Those men today that we buried. The ones you—" She broke off and her head came up and the blue eyes leveled at him. "I am not as great as Martinius. I am weaker. But also I am more practical. I know the need for protection, for being armed when there is trouble. Words won't always help, not even good words from the Bible—so I must tell you something."

"Go ahead." It was spellbinding just watching her lips move.

"When you turn in, you'll find their guns and cartridge belts on the floor of the wagon. This is a big country. No telling what we'll run into before we reach Kentucky. I was supposed to bury the weapons with their bodies, but I couldn't—so while Martinius had his back turned, I took them and hid them. Until tonight. He's a good man, but he doesn't understand sometimes. How bad people can be. He's simple like that, sees good in everyone. Even men like those beasts this afternoon.''

"You did right, Edna. Those guns will come in handy. The shotguns aren't enough." Again he was in awe of her.

"I'll talk to Martinius in the morning about what I did. He'll be disappointed in me, but he will understand. I'll tell him I took them for you. You need a weapon.''

"Did you, Edna? Take them for me, I mean?"

"Yes," she said firmly, not turning away this time. "You may as well know now. Martinius wants you to stay with us. To help us. To become a servant of the Lord and help us with our work in Kentucky, spreading the teachings of the Bible."

David Bard did not flinch at that. He smiled, for he had half expected as much. He shook his head at Edna Sunset.

"I figured as much. Like paying for my keep, but I don't mind that. Time enough to talk that one over when he gets us all to Kentucky and we settle in.''

"Just wanted you to know.''

"I'm thanking you for that. And for the guns. I do want them.''

"Then I'm glad we had this talk.''

"I am too." He took a deep breath. "You're powerfully good to look at, Sister Edna.''

"Don't say that—please." The blue eyes widened.

"Why can't I say it when it's true? The truest thing I ever said—Edna—" He reached for her, awkwardly, fearfully, not really knowing if it was the right time or place for such a move.

It wasn't. She had scrambled backwards, risen to her

feet. Her face wasn't angry. Merely colder and somehow expressionless.

"I'll be saying good night, David Bard," she murmured tonelessly. "Please don't talk nice to me like that. Not here, not now, not ever. There is no room in my heart for a man."

"But, Edna, I only meant—"

"I know what you meant." Her thin smile was gloomy. "Good night, David," she whispered and turned away.

He watched her go, with mixed feelings of hurt, confusion, and wonder. And never had she looked more beautiful than by firelight. He saw her roll herself up in another coarse woolen blanket and take her place within a few yards of the campfire, on the flat earth, curled and huddled up like an Indian squaw. Silence fell over the campsite, broken only by an intermittent sputter of twigs from the slowly dying fire. David Bard turned away himself, putting his back to her. He too stared down at the ebbing fire.

There was an awful lot to think about now.

There was no room in his mind for any questions about John Brown and Harpers Ferry. Or slavery in the country.

Somehow that had already become the past.

As if he had been some other man in some other life.

Glory be to God, David Bard reflected.

These people—the preacher and her—

What mess have I gotten myself into this time?

The big, round white moon overhead against a field of a thousand twinkling stars could not have given him an answer. Any kind of answer. David did not need to know the reply to that question.

He was young enough to know that he was headed for trouble. Big trouble, again. Religion didn't go down too easy with a lot of folks who were more likely to blame the Good Lord for their miseries as anyone. Martinius Rheinbeck was going to have his big hands full.

He was also man enough to know that he wanted Sister Edna Sunset the way a man wants a woman. A grown man.

He couldn't call it love because he didn't know what that was.

All he did know was that his body was beginning to fever for her. And the fever didn't get any better the more times he was around her, saw her moving, watched the sway of her hips and the rise and fall of her bosom—God, she was something! Those blue, blue eyes and that long hair like golden corn in the sunlight.

David Bard returned to his pallet in the wagon. He left his old clothes in a pile by the fire so that Martinius Rheinbeck could see them in the morning. And burn them.

Not even the sight of the Tarzy brothers' guns and cartridge belts made him feel any better. She had left them as she had said, by his bedside. The Navy Colt and the horse pistol. Good enough weapons for a man in the wilderness. On any count.

He did not sleep well that October night.

He couldn't.

There was a vision of an angel in his restless slumber.

An angel with cornflower-blue eyes and long hair the color of ripe corn in the sun—with red, red lips and white, white breasts.

The harvest moon shone down on the sleeping camp.

No birds twittered from the surrounding trees.

In far-off Harpers Ferry, John Brown was making his last stand.

Losing everything on his one toss of the dice.

A raid on a United States arsenal.

Outnumbered and outfought, his position was grave.

The shadow of the gallows was beginning to lengthen over his lanky, rawboned form. A shadow in his life since Osawatomie Creek.

Forgive him, O Lord, for he knew not what he did.

That is what Martinius Rheinbeck would have said for him had he had the opportunity.

But he did not.

Martinius Rheinbeck was sleeping the deep untroubled sleep of a man with no guilt on his soul or anger in his brain.

Nearer, my God, to Thee
Nearer to Thee! . . .

Amen to that, Martinius Rheinbeck.

A HOOT AND A HOLLER TO HORSEFALL

The morning brought a change in the climate. A severe one. There were no sun, no clouds, only a gray overcast sky which would have been depressing, save that there wasn't much time to think about the weather. There was far too much to do.

When they broke camp, after a mutually quiet breakfast of coffee and fritters again, Martinius Rheinbeck hitched up the horses silently and motioned David Bard to take his place in the rear of the wagon. David had not yet strapped on the weapons which Sister Edna Sunset had salvaged for him. Time enough for that along the trail. The girl herself said nothing to him beyond a morning greeting. He felt just fine despite a troubled sleep. All of his stiffness from his assortment of abrasions was on the wane. Even his shoulder felt less constricted. The buckskin outfit with matching hat made him far more presentable to the eye.

He sensed that, knew it to be a fact, and in that knowledge lay a wealth of feeling good. He knew he was a far more respectable figure than the bloody wretch who had come reeling out of the forest two days ago. Martinius Rheinbeck's eyes were mutely approving, if a shade dubious about something. David did not question him but dutifully took his place in the wagon after checking the water supply in the barrels lashed to the sides of the Conestoga. He also reloaded the shotgun he had used on the Tarzys. As Martinius guided the horses with murmured commands and directional pulls on the reins, David examined the arsenal of the men he had killed, the gift from Edna Sunset. The Navy Colt was in prime condition; it had been kept oiled and cleaned. The horse pistol was of more ancient vintage. A frontier model which had seen better days. Still, it was yet serviceable and as such more valuable than hard money out here in the vast wilderness where every tree, every boulder, every turn in the road, might harbor danger. David was more than a little glad that Sister Edna had done what she had. You never could have too many weapons in unfamiliar territory. Which this was. He had never been this far West before and was admiring of Rheinbeck's steady progress forward, as if he knew exactly where they were headed.

He pulled the Bowie knife up from the floorboards, wiped it clean, and placed it under the pallet for the time being. Later he would think about fashioning a sheath for it so he could carry it on one of the two gunbelts. He had decided on the Colt for his main piece. It was much the better of the two sidearms.

The grayness of the sky did not abate and the trail got no less difficult. Now there was only furrowed roadway, with treacherous dips and bends. The forest had thinned, however, and the four horses picked up their pace at Rheinbeck's urging, as if smelling the flatlands that lay ahead. Virginia sloped and rolled in many places, but Kentucky was much flatter, not counting the mountain ranges to the north. Martinius Rheinbeck pushed on, handling the reins all that morning, with Edna Sunset positioned at his side. They had hardly spoken to each other since sunup. David wondered if it was their usual procedure, thinking it might have something to do with her disobeying his wishes about the dead men's guns. He suspected as much, and soon enough he had his answer.

It came all at once, with a hawk making a lazy flight in the gray sky as the Conestoga reached a sharp turn in the road.

"No need to punish yourself, Sister Edna," Martinius Rheinbeck said suddenly, not turning to her. "You did what you thought was right. I can have no quarrel with that."

"It was not easy to cross you, Brother Martinius."

"Aye—I know that, too. Will it help, girl, if I tell you that perhaps you were right? In this godless world, we may well have need of the tools of outlaws and ruffians and sinners. In any event, the young man who is our guest will certainly make good use of them."

David could hear the joyful relief in Edna Sunset's response to Rheinbeck's tolerance of what she considered a fault, in spite of the motives that had led her astray.

"Oh, Martinius—do you truly mean what you say?"

"I do indeed. Let's leave the matter there, girl."

"Thank you, Martinius. And bless you."

''God willed you to flout my wishes, Sister. We will see the wisdom in the act. Sooner or later.''

Once more David Bard had to admire the manner in which they spoke to one another. Almost holy talk, he would have called it, though he had not known many religious teachers in his life. But the formal speech, the clear words, the courtesy they showed one another, were something to see and hear.

He decided not to say anything himself, as if he had not heard them parlay. It might be better that way. It was their business and not his. So he remained silent.

Until the next halt for the moon meal.

Martinius Rheinbeck pulled the Conestoga off the road into another clearing. This one did not serve the shelter of the other locations. There was nothing but a grove of dogwood trees, their branches naked and their slight trunks offering little in the way of protection. Still, it was the only spot they had come to in a great while. ''Are you well enough to see to the horses, David?''

''Be glad to, Martinius.'' He clambered out of the interior of the wagon as soon as Sister Edna got down from her side. The tall, beautiful woman had not looked his way all morning. ''We still in Virginia? I can't rightly tell.''

''We'll be reaching the border by sundown, David. I calculate we are due north of Gate City and should be seeing the Gap before it's too dark. That will get all of us across the mountains, and then it's a hoot and a holler to Horsefall.''

''Then it's Kentucky tomorrow, sure enough?''

''Sure enough indeed.'' The preacher smiled, stroking his black, triangular beard. ''See to those horses now.''

David Bard did as he was told.

*   *   *

After the noonday meal, they sat about, resting, to allow the food to digest. There was little variety to the meals, but at least the grub was nourishing. Sister Edna was a fair hand with a frying pan and she seemed to have several ways to make corn fritters and beans tastier. A dash of molasses pepped them up considerably. Martinius and David rested their backs against the grove of dogwood trees. Edna Sunset walked off to be by herself. Martinius Rheinbeck watched her with affection in his dark brown eyes. David saw his expression and spoke almost reflexively.

"She's a mighty fine girl, Martinius."

"Aye. That she is. The Lord sent her to me when I needed her the most. She's my only kin on this earth. I never had any children of my own."

"Why didn't you ever marry, Martinius? Is it against your religion?"

"No, David. We are allowed to marry. But it is not for me. It would not be fair to ask any woman to share the hardships and the daily toil of a preacher-man. You see what it is like."

There was nothing else to say to that. David leaned back against his own dogwood tree and shook his head.

"Wish this old dogwood was bigger. Can hardly accommodate my back. They never do grow very high, do they?"

Martinius Rheinbeck stared at him strangely. The dark brown eyes seemed to glow. With religious fervor.

"Then I take it, David Bard, that you do not know or have never heard the legend of the dogwood tree?"

"Can't say that I have, Martinius. Is there one?"

"There is indeed. It is a beautiful legend." Martinius

Rheinbeck stared up at the gray sky now, his head tilted, his back to his dogwood. "Listen carefully. And remember all that I tell you. At the time of the crucifixion of the Son of our Lord, the dogwood had been the size of the oak and other trees of the forest. It was a very strong and firm tree. So its timber was used for the cross that the Son carried up Golgotha. The dogwood tree never forgave itself for its being used for such a cruel thing. Jesus, nailed upon the dogwood, sensed this feeling. In his compassion for all forms of sorrow and suffering, he took pity on the dogwood. And there on the spot decided that never again would the dogwood grow so strong and tall to be used as a cross again. *Henceforth,* said the Son, *you shall be bent and slender and twisted and your blossoms shall be in the form of a cross . . . two long and two short petals. And in the center of the outer edge of each petal there will be nail prints, brown with rust and stained with red, and in the center of the flower will be a crown of thorns, and all who see it will remember. . . .* That, David, is the legend of this tree and why it will never grow big and tall again. Not ever."

David stared at him wonderingly.

"Sweet Jesus, is that all true?"

"It is as true as the Word, my son. Believe it."

Turning, David ran his hand over the slender trunk of his tree. "I wish there were blossoms now so I could see for myself. About that shape of a cross—I never did notice that before."

"It is there," Martinius Rheinbeck said, with great faith, "for those that can see it."

"I'll see it," David avowed, firmly. "Come spring again."

"Will you remember the legend as I told it to you? For you will pass the story on one day. It will be your duty."

"I'll remember, Martinius. I swear I will."

"Good. I accept your oath, David Bard. Now let's continue on the route to the Lord's work, my son."

They got to their feet just as Sister Edna Sunset came back from her lonely walk. David crossed the area quickly so that he could hand her up to her place behind the horses. She tried to demur, but he insisted. And when his hand encircled her pliant waist as he hoisted her up, he could feel the sensation clear through her cotton dress. He knew that she was aware of him. After last night she would have been a simpleton if she did not know just how he felt. How much he longed for her.

"Thank you, Brother David."

"You're welcome, Sister Edna."

He was not deaf to her sudden formality.

Smiling tightly, he mounted himself and took his place behind them once more. He patted Martinius Rheinbeck on one broad shoulder. "Tomorrow I handle the reins for a spell, Martinius. It's high time I was doing something around here besides watering the animals. And eating up all your provisions."

"As you wish, David. You should be strong enough by then."

"I'll be strong enough. You can bet on that."

"I do not bet, but I accept your assurances in the spirit in which they are given. HO—THERE!" Martinius Rheinbeck gently flicked the bullwhip curled at his side for a driver's use. The four horses bridled, then stirred themselves, pulling the wagon out slowly from its shelter off the roadway.

The weather had worsened. The skies had grown darker
still. There was a threat of a rainstorm in the air. The
southerly wind had risen in intensity. There was a mild
blow buffeting at them now, fanning across their faces and
garments. Martinius Rheinbeck tugged the wide brim of
his conically crowned hat down. Edna Sunset took her
long, golden hair and braided it into a tight knot so that it
hung more heavily at her back. The horses whinnied and
snorted in the gusts but pushed on dutifully, mindful of the
preacher's resonant voice of command and the light flick
of the bullwhip. Ahead, the trail led toward a flat, treeless
plain of about a thousand yards in circumference. Martinius
Rheinbeck drove the team of horses toward that. David
Bard asked about the bare plain.

"It is one of the landmarks that tells me I am on the
right road. That open area is Massacre Flats. Where a
wagon train of settlers heading West were slaughtered by a
band of Shawnees who had come further east in search of
new land. The settlers saw the paint and feathers and
lost their heads. They opened fire. The Shawnees answered back. That happened more than twenty years ago,
David, but it has never been forgotten. Don't be surprised
if you see a few bones out there."

"I won't be," David said, "but I won't like seeing
anything like that. I never did."

"Amen to that, boy," Martinius Rheinbeck muttered.

The storm that was in the wind and the air broke just as
they were halfway across Massacre Flats. The skies blackened like magic; the atmosphere shook with violence and
thunder. And then the rain came down. In sweeping tor-
rents, a deluge. A battering, splashing, driving rain which
drove the terrified horses forward with all the speed they

could muster. Rheinbeck had no need for the whip, nor was there any place to go but dead ahead. When they finally reached the shelter of the forest beyond Massacre Flats, the damage had been done. They were all thoroughly drenched and soaked to the skin—even David, who had tried to help, refusing to stay within the cover of the wagon.

Rheinbeck parked the wagon under a thick canopy of gigantic oaks. The thunder had gone and the lightning had lessened; now there was only oceans of water, coming down in literal waterfalls.

"The wrath of God," Martinius Rheinbeck murmured, "dropping down from the heavens to remind us how weak and mortal we are."

Edna Sunset, moisture stippling her exquisite face, shuddered.

"Blessed be the rain, Martinius, for it nourishes the earth and makes all things grow."

"Even so, child, even so."

"Whatever it is," David Bard smiled grimly, "it's just about the wettest rain I ever did see."

There was no argument about that. There couldn't be. Martinius Rheinbeck had not been present at the deluge in the Bible, nor had he been with Noah and his family on the ark. So he kept his peace.

And they all waited for the rain to stop, huddling together in the big Conestoga wagon while the horses pawed the wet earth restlessly and the heavens cried, seemingly endlessly.

They had come a long, long way.

But the journey was not yet done.

For which David Bard, close enough to the form of

Sister Edna Sunset, with all her dampened beauty emitting an aroma that was somehow like perfume, was extremely grateful.

Good had come out of bad as far as he was concerned.

And even with all the pounding rain, so thick you could barely see fifty feet, the world seemed a beautiful place indeed.

Where all things might be possible.

Including the love of a wondrous sweet woman.

Sister Edna Sunset.

The most extraordinary female he had ever known.

Not counting Ma.

God bless her.

God bless them both.

The fort at Harpers Ferry had at last been forced open.

John Brown and the pitiful last of its defenders fell back before the entrance of Colonel Robert E. Lee and his trained soldiers. The carnage of the arsenal's interior was mute evidence of the terrible cost to Brown and his men. The wounded and the dying were now totally helpless. All the fight had gone out of them. The date was the eighteenth of October, eighteen hundred and fifty nine. A day that would be long remembered, now.

Colonel Lee stepped forward, trim, military, handsome. He approached the defeated Ohio insurrectionist and halted a few feet before him. "John Brown," he declared clearly and carefully. "I arrest you in the name of the United States Government and henceforth will hold you and your men in custody until the chosen time when you shall be turned over to the proper authorities for trial. What say you, John Brown, to these charges of sedition against duly elected federal authority?''

John Brown's craggy, white-bearded face stiffened resolutely. He straightened erect and raised the short, peculiar sword, extending it to Robert E. Lee. Hilt first.

''Your prisoner, sir.'' His sorrowful smile, though bleak, was yet defiant. ''I shall leave it to the people to judge the right or wrong of my act. You will see to my wounded, sir?''

''Of course,'' Lee said firmly. In his handsome face was a rather grudging admiration for this tall, bearded lunatic who had taken on the whole U.S. government and made them answer his rash act.

John Brown placed his palms together and bowed his head.

''Thank you, Colonel. Bless you in the name of the Lord.''

Thus history had been made again.

The name of Harpers Ferry was emblazoned in the record books forever. Military and otherwise. The first giant undertaking by those who would oppose slavery and do something about it. Like that other huge gun sounded in the anti-slavery war. The Connecticut woman, Harriet Beecher Stowe, had brought forth a novel earlier in the decade. A book called *Uncle Tom's Cabin* and the new England states had come alive with anger and shame, so skillfully and vividly did Mrs. Stowe detail the miserable plight of the Negro in America. Abolitionists and anti-slavers hailed Harriet Beecher Stowe. The South hated her, defiled her name, but the country had been awakened to a condition that had gone on far too long.

John Brown had carried the fight forward.

There was no turning back for America now.

The deed had been done.

As William Shakespeare had once written, the past had become prologue.

And the dogs of war howled and snarled.

WAGON WHEELS AND ROPE FEVER

David Bard strapped Pete Tarzy's cartridge belt around his lean middle. The Navy Colt rode easily in the leather holster. He left the horse pistol and the other belt in the wagon where it would be readily available if needed. Martinius Rheinbeck refused to put that belt on. With a sad smile he rejected David's offer to do so. When the heavy rain had at last subsided and the huge Conestoga moved out once more, the first concern had been drying out. Everyone and everything was thoroughly drenched and sodden. So the preacher decreed an immediate camp to the other side of Massacre Flats. There Sister Edna built a small fire and they all gathered about it, appreciating its warmth and comfort. No one was particularly hungry, but a pot of coffee went well. It was then that, dried out, David remembered the gunbelts. Rheinbeck's story about the Shawnee slaughter of the settlers had reminded him of the hazards and misfortunes that could occur in open country hundreds of miles from any kind of law or justice. Hadn't all of them nearly been killed by the rotten Tarzy brothers?

Martinius Rheinbeck was patient with him.

"Understand me, David. It is well that you are armed. You may even be able to get us some fresh meat. But for myself, I have taught myself never to rely upon weapons of any kind to make my way through this life."

"Have you ever used a gun, Martinius?"

"Many, many times. In truth, I am a fair shot. But that was before I took to the Good Book and its teachings. I have not needed one since."

"Until yesterday," David reminded him. Almost spitefully.

Rheinbeck's smile was gracious.

"As you say. But you will note that Providence placed you in our path and you were there to intercede for Sister Edna and I. You see? It was ordained that you should come to us as you did."

"You sure beat the argument, don't you?" David laughed, a mite sarcastically. "Never met a body who thinks the way you do, Martinius. You really do believe there is good in everybody, don't you?"

Sister Edna stirred before the older man could answer.

"We must think that way, David Bard, or there is no hope at all for the work we are setting out to do."

The preacher beamed approvingly.

"Well spoken, Sister Edna. There, David, do you see the wisdom of such thinking?"

David shrugged. "You both got me beat. All I can say is we'll do it your way until my way becomes right necessary." He pushed back the buckskin hat from his damp brow. "Anyhow, there's nothing wrong with the coffee. It's better'n medicine."

The dark clouds had lightened, even though it was drawing toward evening. Martinius Rheinbeck consulted his timepiece. He grunted. "It would be better that we made the border before sundown. There will be a creek there. A running stream which would make for a good campsite. Should be about another two hours on the trail. What say you both to that—?"

"I'll take the reins this time," David Bard said authoritatively. "No arguments. It's my turn."

Rheinbeck's white teeth gleamed from the forest of beard.

"Done, David Bard. Sister Edna will ride up front with you. I should like to restore myself a little. I am tired."

And so it was done.

David Bard moved the Conestoga out, feeling glad to hold the reins and taking charge in a way. It made him feel older and less the boy. What was better, far better, he had the pleasure of Edna Sunset at his side, sitting so close to him on the platform that her curved hip was touching his own. The sensation was as nice as he expected it to be. But she said nothing and merely stared at the trail ahead, her arms folded in her lap. The long, flaxen hair still tied in a knot trailed down her lovely back.

"Giddyap there—*har!*"

The four horses seemed to recognize a new hand, another leader. The lead horses whickered, snorted, and moved out with sudden vigor. The Conestoga gained the worn roadway, following in the path of the-Lord-only-knew how many countless wagons that had passed this way before. Somewhere off to the right an animal howled. Sister Edna Sunset huddled against David, almost unthinkingly.

"Just a critter," David said softly. "Wolf or dog, maybe. Nothing for us to worry about. Bears don't sound like that."

"Oh," she said, and drew back to her position. But her thigh still touched his own. "It was such a terrible cry."

"That it was. But it wasn't for us."

Martinius Rheinbeck, sitting cross-legged on the pallet which had served as David's bed, was studying his Bible, the thick, dog-eared book lying opened on his knees. His lips moved silently.

Horsefall was now but thirty-eight miles away.

It seemed that the long journey would end without further event. But it was not to be. The Lord, who moved in the mysterious ways that Martinius Rheinbeck was always ready to point out, had yet another mammoth ordeal with which to try them, for all of Rheinbeck and Sister Edna's faith and unswerving conviction about the good in man—and David Bard's natural skepticism and hostility about people, which had begun for him with the senseless slaying of his father by a drink-crazed soldier he hardly knew.

The hour was bearing down on five o'clock when the huge Conestoga wagon circled a jagged pile of rock and came into one more clearing. And David Bard tugged on the reins hard and lifted his voice in a shout to the four horses. The wheels, with the hand brake applied, grated to a full stop. They could not go on now.

Before them lay a tableau not one of them had ever

witnessed. Something often heard about but mercifully beyond their personal experience—until this very moment.

A hanging was in progress.

A lynching, a necktie party, a rope dance—all the vulgar names given such a lawless act by the self-appointed righteous ones who would not wait for a judge and a jury to hear the evidence that would make certain the right man was about to be hanged. Or woman. Posses and vigilante committees alike were guilty of such barbarism—against innocent and guilty both. Far too often it was an innocent wretch who dangled at the end of the rope. It didn't seem to matter as long as *somebody* was hanged.

This somebody was a man.

A black man. A Negro. As terrified as the nearness of death can make a man. Surrounded by at least a dozen horsemen, all crowding him, pushing him ahead of their mounts, toward a tall, solitary oak tree, standing stark and naked, apart from a nearby grove of similar trees. But this was a hanging tree. One huge, gnarled limb extended outward from the withered trunk, a full twelve feet above the ground. The Negro was whimpering and the men were hooting derisively, snarling down at him, poking him along with their rifle barrels and pistols. Kicking him, too.

The determined group was no more than thirty yards from where David Bard had jerked the leaders to a halt. Martinius Rheinbeck needed no urging. He towered behind David and Edna Sunset and from the interior of the wagon, his great stentorian voice boomed:

"STOP YOU GODLESS MEN! IN THE NAME OF THE GOOD LORD, I COMMAND YOU TO PUT ASIDE YOUR HATE AND LACK OF REASON! YOU MUST

NOT DO THIS TERRIBLE THING WHICH IS EVIL IN
THE SIGHT OF JEHOVAH!''

David Bard had never admired a man so much in his life
as he did Martinius Rheinbeck at that precise moment in
the scheme of things. But he was fearful, too. Lynching
parties would hang anybody if they got it into their heads.
Hanging was a contagious disease. Once started, it might
not stop.

''Martinius, don't rile them,'' David muttered. ''This
ain't any of our business.''

''All men are our business,'' the preacher said with
quiet force. ''Come. Dismount with me. I will show you
how the word of God can turn men away from their worser
natures.''

Whatever he might accomplish, he had already achieved
a victory. The lynch party now had turned in their saddles
in the direction of the booming voice. Even the black man
was stunned into silence. The tableau held. ''Remain with
the wagon, Sister Edna. David and I will see to this,''
Rheinbeck ordered, dropping to the earth and straightening, adjusting his conical, wide-brimmed hat. David joined
him, now more glad than ever that he had strapped on Pete
Trazy's Navy Colt. Better armed than not.

The preacher and his young partner walked toward the
waiting horsemen. As the sky grew darker still and a horse
made pawing noises with its hooves, Edna Sunset murmured, ''God go with you both. . . .I will pray for
you. . . .''

David Bard was more than certain they were going to
need God and all the help they could get. This was no
strawberry festival. Never had he seen a ring of faces so
dead set on hanging a man. Any man. They all looked so

mean and ugly. As he and the preacher drew closer, he tried to spot a sheriff's badge or a marshal's shield, but none were to be seen. Sometimes the only law officer for many miles around was a United States marshal and it wasn't easy for one man to police such a large territory. That was one of the reasons mere citizens like these got it into their fool heads to take the law into their own hands.

But, hell, Martinius had said they were pretty darn close to Horsefall and the town ought to have a sheriff—unless this bunch had rode in from somewhere else.

There was no more time to think about that. None at all.

They were face-to-face with the horsemen now.

No more than twenty feet away from them.

And Martinius Rheinbeck was taking his stand.

"Who is in command here?" he asked with forceful clarity. And even before his powerful voice finished, a raucous angry query came back from the massed riders. "Who in hell wants to know?"

"A servant of the Lord, my friend. One who has been placed in your path this day to prevent you from doing a terrible thing you will regret the rest of your days."

Another voice, sarcastic and vicious, hurled more words back at him. "Says you, preacher-man. This tar baby is gonna get what's coming to him!"

"Thou shalt not kill. Judge not lest ye be judged yourselves. What is this man's fault?" The fearlessness and solemn implacability of Martinius Rheinbeck had its effect. As it always did and would. Someone in the mob muttered, "What are we all waitin' on? Let's do what we come to do. I gotta field to plough in the mornin'. Ridin' around after this blamed coon all day—let's hang him and be done with it." A roar of agreement swept over the

horsemen. But no one moved to propel the Negro to the hanging tree. The coiled length of rope in the hands of the rider close to him was already fashioned in the traditional hangman's noose. David Bard was not blind to the Negro's condition, either. He had been beaten and his clothes torn from his body so that he was very nearly naked in the remainder of his ragged shirt and pants. He wore no shoes, and even his feet left bloodstains in the hard brown earth. David said nothing. But he kept his eyes on the men before him and Rheinbeck, and his hand hovered near the butt of the Navy Colt, ready to use if it need be. Hostility was here.

"You have not yet told me what crime this man has committed. Or are you merely yielding to your hatred of your black brother—that would be a far greater crime." Rheinbeck would not back down.

"Stop jawin' about things you don't know!" a rider in the forefront of the horsemen bellowed angrily. "This negrah helped hisself to a horse that weren't his. Jim Frigg's horse."

"And where is the animal now? I see no riderless horse."

"The mare musta thrown the darky—we caught him on foot just a mile back there."

"So you never saw this man on the animal?"

"What's that got to do with it? Couldn't be anyone but him. This boy's the only one coulda stolen that mare! Name's Ben Parks. No-good no-account—one of them slaves from the Johnson farm—he been tryin' to run away since he was old enough to walk."

Martinius Rheinbeck shook his head, sure of himself now.

"Then no one saw him steal the mare or ride upon its back. You have no proof, no evidence. You cannot hang this man. And above all, you cannot take the law into your own hands. Return him to your courts, let a jury decide his innocence or guilt. Hang him and the sin will be on your souls for all eternity. There is judgment in Heaven, my friends. Do you wish to be found wanting when your day comes?" He roved his penetrating gaze at the men before him.

The words hit home, for all of their malicious intent upon hanging a black man. Besides, now there were witnesses to what they wanted to do. A preacher, a young fellow, and some woman back there with the wagon and the horses. A low grumbling muttering ran through the crowd. The horseman with the rope looked surprised and scowled angrily at his companions.

"You gonna let this Bible-spouter talk you outa what we been fixin' to do since sunup? C'mon, where's your sand? Ben Parks knows he stole that horse; we know it and Jim Frigg says it has to be him, so let's get on with it." As if to give them courage, he spurred his mount toward the hanging tree, slowed beneath the long crooked strong limb, and let sail his rope. It snaked upward, cleared the limb, and came down, trailing into his ready hand. The noose was ready.

David Bard rested his right hand on his gun butt.

"I'd be listening to what the preacher is telling you," he said very quietly. "He's right, you know. None of you got any call hanging a man. It's up to the law to do that. You'll only get yourselves a pile of trouble if you hang this poor colored boy."

"Who're you?" came a growl from the crowd of

horsemen. "Some gunfighter hired to do the preacher's shootings for him?"

"I'm no gunfighter. I'm Martinius Rheinbeck's friend. And I believe in the Good Book same as he does and in people treating each other fair and square same as he does. That good enough for you?"

Martinius Rheinbeck was quick to seize the opening that David's speaking up had provided. "Do as we advise you. Take the black boy back to town with you. Let him be tried. Gather the evidence. Your hands will be freed of all responsibility and guilt. You will have behaved like Christians. If this man has coveted his neighbor's goods, he has broken one of the Commandments. And should be punished."

He had swayed them, if only to plant a seed of doubt in their minds so that not one of them could now in all conscience or good faith go through with what had seemed a fine idea in the morning. But now, despite all of Martinius Rheinbeck's good work in the name of God, fear and unreason destroyed all that he had accomplished with his cautionary, wise words.

The uncertainty, the haggling words, his own lack of any schooling, did the poor Negro youth in. Unable to read into what was being said about him and with all eyes turned away from him while the preacher-man held the center of the stage, he bolted and ran. Pell-mell for the forest which beckoned with shelter and protection from these mounted riders who would hang him. It was the unwisest move he would ever make. To simple minds, flight means guilt—it is tantamount to a confession.

Whatever it was, it was enough to make one man of that mounted mob go into instant action. As the desperate black man dashed in a headlong flight for the woods, a shot rang out. A single rifle shot. It cracked across the clearing with a high keen of sound. And at the end of the sound, the black man went down, with the back of his head torn clean off by a heavy bullet from a long rifle.

Ben Parks was as dead as if he had been hanged.

Silence fell over the group of horsemen until the man who had used his rifle growled: "Innocent fellers don't run, do they? Wal, that's one horse thief we don't have to worry about no more."

"You did right, anyway you look at the thing, Clem. Reckon we ought to string the body up anyways. Good thing for other horse thieves to see. And nigger boys too big for their britches."

The rider closest to him had spoken, and now all the others flung one last look at Martinius Rheinbeck. And were startled into another long silence. Never in any of their mean lives would they ever see again a face as unforgettably contemptuous as this one was.

The preacher's hawk nose was quivering as though it were alive; his dark brown eyes were very nearly twin pools of blazing anger. His great hands had knotted into rigid, clenched fists. His entire form was caught up in some whirlpool of inner fury that he was obviously fighting valiantly to control with every logical ounce of his mind and body. David Bard stood ready to go into action, willing to take his cue from anything Martinius Rheinbeck wanted to do. He would draw in an instant if he had to. His own shock and quick remorse at the sudden murder of the Negro, for murder was what it was, was now shunted aside in his concern for Martinius Rheinbeck, who, he was beginning to realize, was a very special kind of man. A one-of-a-kind person.

With a great effort the tall, bearded giant checked himself. Subsiding, he glared at the circle of horsemen. When he spoke again, the damning words were clear, concise, and to the mark. "May God have mercy on your heartless souls. I will not. Come, David. I cannot abide the company of godless men."

They walked back to the wagon where Sister Edna Sunset awaited them anxiously. Her compassionate eyes spoke volumes about what she had just witnessed. Martinius Rheinbeck and David Bard did not look back once. They had left a stunned almost shameful lynch mob who were now not too sure that they had behaved well at all. But such is the nature of such men that soon enough someone made a ribald remark, another laughed, and a third one suggested they do something about the notion of stringing Ben Parks' corpse to the limb of the hanging tree—which they set about doing as fast as they could ride to the place where the unfortunate slave had fallen. "Those damn holy rollers," a moon-faced rider opined, "all they ever do is try to talk other folks outa doing things that have to be done! Ain't a real man among 'em. . . ."

"He was somethin', though. Never did see a face like that. And did you hear him . . . like it was the Lord himself talkin'!"

They didn't want to think about that, so they didn't.

"Hell's bells—if Ben didn't steal that horse, who did?"

No one had an answer for that, either.

Horse thievery was the greatest crime in a country that was growing. Not even killing a man was on a level with that one. A man needed his horse to survive, the further west he got.

*   *   *

The heavy Conestoga wagon pulled out, leaving the scene that David Bard would always remember. Wordlessly, Martinius Rheinbeck took the reins. David Bard did not attempt to stop him. Sister Edna Sunset remained silent, also. She knew the preacher better than David did. None of them cared to look back, so they did not see the dangling, twisting corpse of a young Negro with his head blasted to ruin, swaying from the limb of the hanging tree. The band of vigilante horsemen rode off in the way they had come, from the opposite direction. Maybe they had come from Gate City; maybe they hadn't. It did not matter. What mattered, obviously, was that a poor wretch, innocent or guilty, had been murdered out of hand. And all of Martinius Rheinbeck's faith and wisdom was shaken. Faith in himself, the Good Lord, and the goodness of men. David somehow sensed that. Knew it for a truth. And in the knowing, his heart and admiration went out once more to this sometimes foolhardy preacher-man.

"Martinius," he said suddenly from the depths of the wagon.

"Yes, David?" Rheinbeck did not turn around, keeping his eye on the darkening trail, watching for the proposed campsite where there was a creek of running water. Edna Sunset stared dead ahead, as was her custom. The border was the next consideration.

"I'm that proud to know you, Martinius Rheinbeck."

For a long moment there was no answer.

Then the deep voice said very humbly and softly: "I am obliged to you for that, David."

There were no more words coming. Nothing left to say.

The Conestoga wagon forged on, heading into the gathering darkness of evening. There would be no moon or stars this night. The heavens were miserably overcast and leaden, making it very difficult to believe that there truly was a blue sky above their vast canopy of grayness. It had been all of a dark, dark day.

But Sister Edna Sunset smiled at David Bard, turning to acknowledge what he had just confessed to Martinius Rheinbeck.

A smile not easily forgotten.

A smile that warmed David Bard.

Somehow lightening all the darkness and the sense of sorrow.

The wagon wheels kept on turning, drawing them closer to Horsefall and Martinius Rheinbeck's appointed task.

Spreading the gospel throughout a land that sorely needed the words and wisdom of the Holy Bible. Religion had come to the frontier almost before the white settlers arrived. Catholic and Protestant missionaries had laid the groundwork for the teachings of the Lord. But when new settlements grew far from the missions and people could not travel to hear their preacher or minister or priest, those people then had to rely on traveling preachers. Circuit riders—to perform religious services, whatever the denomination. And it did not stop there, for when these men of good faith arrived in any town, they would preach services, conduct marriages, baptize, set up Sunday schools for the children, and all in all, serve a vital function for settlers who could not do without their chosen God. Thus, Martinius Rheinbeck.

Yet David Bard knew that none of all that would mean a thing without a good gun to back things up.

The frontier was still too uncivilized, too wild, and literally overflowed with bad people. Outlaws, ruffians,

skunks, and just plain snakes. He aimed to provide that
gun for Martinius Rheinbeck, if only the preacher would
let him.

God willing.

There was nothing like a .44 to put some teeth into the
Good Book. And back to an argument.

Render unto Caesar the things which are Caesar's . . .

Just like John Brown had said.

Render unto God the things that are God's. . . .

Martinius Rheinbeck believed with all his heart and
soul. There was room enough for both kinds of thinking if
a man knew when to apply either rule of behavior.

David Bard was sure now that he knew the difference.

They finally reached the border, where the rolling ground
of western Virginia touched the flatter lowlands of Kentucky. The creek with the running fresh water, though
there was no moon, was clearly visible nestling within a
circle of stately pines. The clear stream let off a glistening
glow that guided them. The hour was later than the preacher
had desired, but no harm done. They had reached the first
important leg of the journey. They bedded down for the
night, too exhausted and disheartened even to build a fire
for some coffee and food.

David gave the Conestoga bed back to Martinius
Rheinbeck and Sister Edna Sunset. He had felt guilty
about hogging the wagon and now he could make amends.
It was his turn to sleep on the hard earth. So he did, glad
for the warm buckskin garments and a heavy woolen
blanket. He closed his eyes with the howling of a loon off
somewhere in his ears. It was a comforting sound somehow, for it told of life in this vast wilderness and emptiness.

So he slept, not knowing, as Martinius Rheinbeck and Sister Edna Sunset did not know, that there was a stranger in their midst. Sleeping on the other side of the creek, stretched out as if he were dead under the stark shadow of another hanging tree. A very strange man, indeed.

One none of them was ever going to forget.

THY WILL BE DONE

They saw him in the light of the new morning, and his sudden appearance on the far shore of the creek was rather startling. He waved an arm in greeting and then came long-striding across the knee-deep running stream. He was carrying a huge knapsack on his back, but that was as nothing compared to his appearance. His beard was wild and tangled, his long, uncut hair falling in a heap to his broad shoulders. The clothes he wore were those of a workman or a ferryboat skipper. The pale overhead sunlight, for the dark clouds had given away to blue skies once more, shone down on a hatless head. He was not a tall man, but something about him gave off the illusion of size and strength. Martinius Rheinbeck, Sister Edna Sunset, and David Bard, grouped about the breakfast campfire, enjoying their hot coffee, were caught almost flat-footed.

David went for the Colt in his holster, but Martinius Rheinbeck stayed his hand with a gentle admonition.

"He comes in peace, David. Can you not tell?"

The stranger stamped from the waters, smiling broadly, his bright eyes sweeping over them in instant approval. He shook the stream from his long legs and almost bowed in Sister Edna Sunset's fully heartwarming direction. He allowed the knapsack to fall to the earth and rubbed his hands together, as though he were cold. But it wasn't that at all. The man exuded cheeriness and well-being, as if he and nature were at one and he considered the great outdoors paradise enough.

"Happy morning to you all," the stranger boomed in a voice of unequaled animation. "It is a pleasure to see people again. May I venture to ask for some of that hot coffee? It would go well on this cool morn. And as we are fellow wayfarers in this vast, untamed land, I would be greatly obliged if you do not refuse me. You seem like Christian folk or do my eyes deceive me?"

"They do not." Martinius Rheinbeck smiled, recognizing a mutually well-read man. "David, a cup for our gentleman caller. Sister Edna—some bacon, if you will."

"No, no," the stranger demurred with another toothy smile. "Coffee is all I require. Nectar of the gods in open country. For me, at least." Nodding, he took the tin cup that a wary David Bard handed to him. Like all simple men, David was always uneasy and on guard when in the company of a smooth-talking man. Lawyers and gamblers always talked like this one—he kept his hand near the butt of the Navy Colt as the newcomer sipped grandly from the tin cup. He noted with some satisfaction that Sister Edna wasn't all too convinced, either. There was doubt in her blue eyes.

"Ah, someone in this camp knows how to make coffee—the fair lady, I trust. Congratulations, heartfelt, dear beauty."

The casualness of the compliment, spoken entirely without guile, made Edna murmur, "You are too kind, sir."

"Call me not that, dear lady. It is an appellation I detest. For all the men I have known who were so designated by the society in which they moved were more loutish than I ever was. I am known as Whitman—erstwhile man of letters, journalist, editor—and now I walk this land in search of truths I could not find in the cities . . . but come—tell me of wagon life. I treasure the company and conversation of people such as yourselves. Not bound to their chairs and a humdrum daily existence. You are greater adventurers than you would ever imagine!"

Martinius Rheinbeck had let him speak, shrewdly measuring the man as he voiced these curious sentiments. He liked what he saw and heard. "Whitman, you come at an opportune moment. We are on our way to Horsefall, where I shall set up a tabernacle in the wilderness. We have been without any news for days and you seem to have wandered the country. Surely, you have some tidings for us?"

Whitman's quiet smile was nearly rueful.

"A man of God, then. You look the part, my friend. And the dear lady and Young Buckskins there—are they also purveyors of the Good Book?" The remark was without malice, so Martinius Rheinbeck made introductions all around, Whitman acknowledging each name with a nod of his unkempt head. His untidiness spoke not so much of dirt and shabbiness but more of unconcern for his appearance, for his teeth were very white and his broad hands clean and without calluses. He was clearly no ordinary laborer or farmer.

"So you would venture to Horsefall, is that it? Well, you will be needed there. The town is still growing and there is use for religion. Whatever kind it may be. I paused there for a day's occupation last month and then pushed on. Now I am making it back East. I have seen what I have wanted to see of the frontier. Bold will be my pen and knowledgable my mind as I set down my impressions on paper."

"You a newspaper fellow?" David asked, feeling he had been silent too long and needed to assert himself.

"I committed that great crime once, Apollo. I will not commit it again. So now I write what I feel like writing— and leave gossip and conjecture and criticism and tragedy to others. I am a free soul and choose to remain one as long as I can."

"Apollo?" David echoed, almost dumbly.

Martinius Rheinbeck chuckled. "He is likening you to a Greek god, David. For you are indeed manly and hand-some, as Sister Edna is much like the beauties of the Old Testament."

Whitman beamed. "One man in a hundred would have known that in this illiterate land. My congratulations, Rheinbeck."

"Accepted. Now, despite your distaste for newspapers, we are sorely in need of some word; we have been out of touch too long. How goes the nation?"

"I must quote Lincoln here, my friend. It yet exists half-slave and half-free. And the railroads continue to build to the West. There is some talk back East of the telegraph extending its powers so that messages could be sent by wire clear across the continent—and perhaps over the oceans.''

"You speak of progress only, Whitman," the preacher chided him. "What of events? Be specific, please."

"*Specific*, ah . . ." The bearded newcomer to their camp tasted the word. "Stunning adjective, that. Synonyms—*explicit, definite*. A fine, poetical word. I think I shall use it in my next—" He broke off, almost apologetically. "Forgive me. I ramble."

"Then be what you call *specific*," David challenged him.

"Very well. I shall. The President calls for a tightening of public resolve on the issue of slavery, and as if to flaunt him, that untidy abolitionist John Brown saw fit to attack the arsenal at Harpers Ferry. Fortunately for the country, he was put down after a siege lasting three days."

"When did this take place, Whitman?" Rheinbeck asked.

"On the day before yesterday, as near as I can calculate. I heard about it when I was in Jonesville. And now I am starting back from God's country to civilization, as it is so-called.''

"Harpers Ferry?" Martinius Rheinbeck muttered in a faraway voice. "We were but a few hours' ride from there then—when it happened. . . ." There was only awe in his tone, not suspicion, but David Bard suddenly buried his face into his coffee cup again. "John Brown is a damned fool to think that force of arms will change anything—it is not the way of the Lord, Whitman. Tell me, was Brown killed in his foolhardy attempt?"

"There were the dead and the wounded," Whitman sighed, refilling his cup from the still-hot pot of coffee.

"But the gallows rope awaits Old Osawatomie John Brown. The proper end for the misguided man, I would say."

David Bard stirred, as if to say something, to shout out his protest, but he kept his lips tightly shut. Sister Edna Sunset sensed the struggle within him, somehow, and suddenly her hand stole to his knee and touched it, leaving a reassuring feeling. Rheinbeck and Whitman did not notice. They were enjoying each other's company too much. For in this vast, uneducated country, how often did one man who had read a lot of books meet another man with similar proclivities. Their talk alone signified two worlds of tremendous education, whether self-taught or not.

"I would be pleased if you called me Martinius, Whitman."

"Done. It too suits you. It is Biblical, proud and not profane—you are well cast as a man of God, Martinius. You have majesty and dignity."

"And you, my friend, are a soothsayer with words. I see that, and hear it, too. What is your given name?"

"Walter, alas. But I no longer allow myself to be called that. I much prefer Walt—it is simple, more direct, and far less constricting."

"I do not know what you mean," Rheinbeck shook his head. "But it is your name and your choice. Walt it shall be."

Sister Edna Sunset murmured, "It is too bad you cannot accompany us to Horsefall. You would be most welcome."

"I know that, Sister Edna, and I greatly appreciate the invitation. But, no—my feet ache for the East now, for places I once knew as a child. Long Island, a place called Brooklyn . . ." The bright eyes saddened. "The docks, the alleyways, the shops—" He shook himself. "I have carpentered, set type for newspapers, taught the children in school—I am in my fortieth year, and it is to be hoped I can yet do something with my life. The country is growing with great leaps and bounds—I should like to grow with it. As the leaves of grass grow all around us, eternally.''

"You will grow, Walt," Martinius Rheinbeck agreed with firm conviction. "It is in your nature. I see that. You see to it that growth remains on the side of the angels, and not Lucifer.''

"Lucifer," repeated Walt Whitman. "Beelzebub, Satan, Fallen Angel, Old Nick, Satan, the Devil—call him what they all will—he exists, Martinius. If not as a solid man, then as a thought. And thoughts are far more dangerous than any man can be. As you so well know, with your Bible and your goodness.''

"Even so, go with God.''

"I'll go with him gladly, Martinius," Walt Whitman chuckled, "but the crux and the nub of the matter is—the whole question really is—will he go with me?''

"He turns aside from no man.''

"Or woman—but Man, who is born of God, has a short time to live—''

"And will live in the house of the Lord forever, amen.''

"I cannot stay with you at your own game, Martinius. But I accept your best wishes with deep gladness and obligation. I will remember your words.''

"Remember them, Walt Whitman. And you cannot go wrong or do wrong to anyone.''

David Bard, who was learning all the time, looked on in wonder, listening to the discourse of these two older men.

Such talk and strange words and ideas expressed so vividly were foreign to his ears. The bad news about John

Brown's failure and fate left him puzzled, however. He was no longer certain how he felt about Brown. Three days ago he would have called anyone plain addled if they had said he would feel this way. So he said nothing, trying to compose his inner thoughts, as the preacher-man and the wanderer traded some more bright notions. Through it all, Sister Edna Sunset sat, as lovely and serene as anyone could be, listening, as the sun rose higher in the sky. A fresh new day was growing too. Unlike the cloudy, rainy, and miserable one of just yesterday.

Finally, Walt Whitman took his leave of them, mounting his big pack on his back, refusing all offers of extra provisions. He shook hands warmly all around, and David was amazed at the strength in his hands. And when the strange figure struck out, disappearing into the thick forest to the northeast, Sister Edna Sunset suddenly exclaimed: "Martinius—David—look here. . . ."

They all saw the yellow foolscap lying on the earth near the campfire, where it would not be missed. Where Walt Whitman had been sitting, but no one could remember him leaving it there. A long sheet of writing paper on which there were handwritten words in ink. The penmanship was large and sprawling and very clear. Edna Sunset seized the paper first and held it up to the light to read it. "Why, it's a poem—he must have left it for us."

"Then read it, Sister Edna," Martinius Rheinbeck declared, closing his eyes as though he were in church.

She did, in a clear, melodious voice:

"It's called 'Song of Myself.' " She cleared her throat, paused a second, and then read aloud:

"I celebrate myself, and sing myself,

And what I assume you shall assume,

For every atom belonging to me as good as belongs to you.

I loafe and invite my soul,

I lean and loafe at my ease, observing a spear of summer grass

A child said *What is the grass*? fetching it to me with full hands,

How could I answer the child?

I do not know what it is any more than he. . . ."

Yr. Obedient Servant
Walt Whitman

Edna Sunset's eyes came up from the sheet of yellow foolscap in her slender fingers. There was a strange light in her eyes. Martinius Rheinbeck wagged his bearded head.

"Aye, Sister Edna. A poet, indeed. Those are fine sentiments. Noble ones. A good man, Walter Whitman."

David Bard confessed to a lack of understanding of the strange words. Poem? Why, it had no rhyme or catchiness to it at all the way it should have—like Sunday prayers did.

"No matter, David." Rheinbeck smiled tolerantly. "We will save the gracious souvenir of our guest's presence and one day I will explain it for you." He stared in the direction that their visitor had gone. "I feel it in my bones. He will be a man heard from one day."

David Bard wanted to hear no more of Walter Whitman.

"I say we'd best be pushing on now. We're just about there, according to what you said, Martinius."

"Just about, my boy. No more than two hours ride, I venture. So let us be off. I am hankering to see my new parish, at that."

"I, too, Martinius," Edna Sunset said fervently. "It would be nice to see some womenfolk again."

They stamped out the remains of the fire, mounted up, and readied themselves for the last leg of the journey. Martinius took the reins and David rode shotgun this time. Sister Edna had been advised to take an inventory of the supplies before they reached Horsefall so Rheinbeck could turn in a proper accounting to the folks who had sent for him. So he would be "recompensed"—there was that word again, David thought—for his expenses in making the long trip from the East.

But before she did so, Sister Edna placed the long sheet of yellow foolscap, folded very carefully, into her personal, knitted handbag, where she seemed to store her valuables. There it would remain until it was needed. In spite of the preacher's objections, David rode with one of the shotguns across his lap.

By some tacit, mutual silent agreement, none of them had once referred to the terrible incident of the day before: the awful death of that poor colored boy at the hands of so-called law-abiding citizens—when not even belief in God had helped Martinius Rheinbeck, or Sister Edna Sunset.

David Bard was just not taking any more chances.

There were still too many folks suffering from lynch fever and too many Tarzy brothers—in this wild, untamed country.

Horsefall might not be much better.

Guns still spoke louder than words.

* * *

The hour was leaning toward one-thirty when they all saw the smoke on the horizon. Awesome, dark smoke, billowing upwards, fanning out in a wide panorama of blinding vapors. A hellish tinge of scarlet edged the smoke, sending violent red flashes spiraling upwards. The Cumberland Mountain range formed a mighty backdrop for all this mammoth shroud of dense, thick, coiling fumes.

Martinius Rheinbeck jerked the reins, halting the horses. He stood up and stared long and hard toward the frightening spectacle before them. "What is it, Martinius—forest fire?"

"No, God help us all!" thundered Rheinbeck in a dumbfounded roar. "That can only be Horsefall; it lies in that direction. It's a fire—it cannot be anything else!"

"Glory be," David Bard muttered, not knowing what to do—or say, for that matter. But Martinius Rheinbeck did. For once he used the bullwhip with lashing authority. And the Conestoga lurched forward; the horses pulled for all their worth, and the wheels spun faster than ever before. The big prairie schooner rolled on swiftly, down a long, winding trail which ended at the very core of all that smoke, all those flames. Beneath the horizon.

Sister Edna Sunset clung to the side of the interior of the wagon as Rheinbeck set a furious pace. The water barrels roped to the wagon rattled, the pots and pans clattered, the tied-down tools banged together, the horses snorted in protest.

Martinius Rheinbeck's bearded lips moved in silent prayer even as he pushed the leaders on with a whipping vengeance.

Horsefall, for that is what it was, was going up in choking smoke and fiery flames.

It was as if the world were ending.

In Kentucky, U.S.A.

LET MY SINNERS GO

The tiny settlement, not much more than a collection of twenty frame shacks equally divided to either side of a narrow dirt street, was a holocaust. Pure and simple. Only the purity and simplicity had tragic, heartbreaking beginnings. Later, much later, when it was learned how the awful fire had started, no one who survived could have said, with conviction, that the colony had not been cursed from the very first day of its birth. But for now, as the heavy Conestoga wagon lumbered to the outer limits of the disaster area, the death of Horsefall was but an hour away. Flame had traveled like wildfire and not one of the twenty low structures had escaped the blaze.

And for the next few hours young David Bard was eye-witness to a miracle. And a miracle man. Never again would he ever doubt or question the true worth of Martinius Rheinbeck. Or deride the Good Book—the Holy Bible.

133

There was nothing mysterious about the way the preacher-man moved when emergency and hard times were at hand.

The men of Horsefall had coped valiantly with the conflagration, forming a bucket brigade, but with no fire department of any kind, the situation was hopeless. The wooden frame shacks went up like matchsticks suddenly ignited, spreading from building to building in no time at all. Worse, the people trapped inside—men, women and children—died with the same speed and destructiveness that characterized a prairie fire. The cries and screams of these poor wretches punctuated the efforts of rescuers. In the end, some two dozen poor souls from Horsefall's population of a mere eighty-five people had perished in the flames and smoke. There was nothing anyone could really do to check the calamity. And at three-thirty in the afternoon of what had begun as a bright fall day, the tiny settlement of Horsefall was ashes. Razed to the very ground itself. The holocaust had been complete.

Yet Martinius Rheinbeck rose like a giant among the fallen of Horsefall—moving from the badly burned to the dying like a constant angel, hovering here with words of comfort, pausing there to assist the dead into the last moment with blessings from his Bible, his great hands clasped, lips saying the words that needed to be spoken. Once he plunged into a flaming shack, emerging with a child in his arms, his face blackened, beard singed. But he took not a moment's respite from his work. Sister Edna Sunset was no less a ministering angel. Helping to bandage the injured, calming the frightened little ones who wailed and bawled in terror. Dazed mothers and stricken wives and sisters and daughters stumbled among the flaming ruins, their faces darkened with disbelief and horror.

Those expressions would not go away when ultimately it was discovered that the fire had begun in Amos Ritter's home when a newfangled kerosene lamp with the tall chimney glass was knocked over by the family dog as he romped with the Ritter children. All had perished in the flames. Five humans and a dog.

The horses and livestock, cows and pigs, chickens and roosters, all fled at the first lick of fire. They might never be recovered again. Meanwhile, whatever the settlers of Horsefall had erected to make for a town was now all gone. Nothing but ashes, charred foundations, and rubble remained. There was no Horsefall anymore, only a blackened patch of earth perhaps three hundred yards in length and maybe one hundred yards across. David Bard had never seen the like of such chaos before. He had helped too, as best he could, heedless of his own safety, but he knew in his heart and soul that Martinius Rheinbeck was the genuine hero. Not once did he pause all that awful afternoon to see to himself. He flitted, like a tall, incredible spirit, where he was needed. A prayer here, blessings there, comforting words, always that. And when at last there was no more to be done, when the final smouldering ember spat with sound and crumpled into still ashes and the good people of Horsefall stood back, gazing forlornly at the shattered remnants of their dream colony, only the wailing and weeping of the living could be heard—those who had been spared by a Divine Providence who had yet not spared others.

Toward sundown the site of the disaster was like some battlefield. But not one left to the victors. Men and women moved like ragged phantoms, searching the wreckage for anything that might be salvaged. Furniture, weapons, food—

sentimental keepsakes such as watches, rings, or lockets—
but there was nothing. The catastrophe and ruination had
been total and complete.

There would never be a boom town called Horsefall
near the border separating Virginia and Kentucky in the
shadow of the Cumberland mountain range. Business pro-
moters selected a site where trails crossed and rivers joined,
then sold lots and hoped for settlers to come in—all to
boom the town; Horsefall had been such a location, lying
as it did beyond the Big Stone Gap, where the state of
Kentucky began. The distant towns of Hazard, Blackey,
and Whitney would have profited from a place like Horsefall.
But now it was not to be. Horsefall would never appear on
any map anywhere. *Ashes to ashes and dust to dust, if the
Indians don't get you, then the weather must . . .* as an old
frontier axiom went.

As though he were God come to earth, the survivors of
the little town flocked to Martinius Rheinbeck's side, recognizing his spiritual and fatherly demeanor. They remembered how the men of the town had spoken about a preacher
coming—they needed one now more than ever. It wasn't a
question of religion being good for the soul and for the
bringing up of the young 'uns, it was a matter of sheer
survival; there was nothing and nowhere to turn, no one to
reach out for except this tall, bearded man with the funny
conical hat, piercingly direct eyes, and deep, soothing
voice. Like Father Abraham, Martinius Rheinbeck became
the man of Horsefall's hour.

The saddened men, the fathers, brothers, and sons, let
him speak for them. So at sundown, with some threescore
bewildered and ruined settlers down on their knees beyond
the blackened smudge that had been Horsefall, Martinius

Rheinbeck held an outdoor service. He stood rearing like a mighty oak, arms outstretched in supplication, and called on God in the heavens to help these poor people begin their lives over again in the light of His divine aid and love. He also delivered the Twenty-Third Psalm in a measured, unforgettable bass voice. One which spread out over the heads of the kneeling multitude and fell upon their hearing as lightly as a falling rain and as surely as thunder and lightning.

Off to his left, David Bard and Edna Sunset stood by the Conestoga, watching and listening. For Edna, it was something she had always known about Rheinbeck; for David, it was but one more revelation about this strange man. All of his words, his meanings, were delivered with such clarity and forceful conviction that David had removed his buckskin hat without being conscious of doing so. Sister Edna's curved and lovely face was never more saintlike as she listened to Rheinbeck. David was never more aware of her utter beauty. But this time his response was not physical—his heart and soul were filling with the warmth of love.

"They're good words, Edna," David whispered to her. "Fine words, but they ain't going to feed these people or get those shacks back up again, are they? Night's coming on—where are these folks aiming to sleep?—and then there's vittles, which they ain't got any of."

"Hush, David," she murmured in answer, without anger. "You wait and see—Martinius will do all those things. He has before."

"I got your word on that, Sister Edna?"

"You have my solemn word, David."

And so David did.

And so Martinius Rheinbeck did, exactly as Sister Edna Sunset had vowed. Before another hour passed and the darkness closed over the settlement that only that day had been Horsefall, Kentucky, a settlement barely six months old.

Amen and Rest In Peace.

With Martinius Rheinbeck, all things were possible under God's blue sky. And with His divine help, of course.

All things both great and small.

A dead town, like the phoenix of Greek mythology, could rise from the ashes.

Martinius Rheinbeck intended that it should.

Whatever provisions and supplies remained in the Conestoga wagon were now unloaded and quickly and fairly distributed among the living. Fifty-nine people were a great many to feed, but for one meal until the morrow when something could be done of a more practical nature, like hunting for game, this would have to serve. And it did. There was enough bacon and corn meal and flour and coffee left that, if properly rationed, could provide for the survivors of Horsefall. The water barrels yet held enough for a tin cup for each person. Sister Edna Sunset, assisted by a battery of eager women who had put aside their grief to see to their living kinfolk, managed to whip up an extraordinary repast, considering the conditions. Fire, ironically, was easy enough to come by—the Devil's own joke!—for smouldering embers still sent up little eddies of flame and smoke wherever the eye could see. So the vast supper was accomplished as night fell and the outer darkness hid the ruins of burned-out Horsefall. Everyone ate in a hard, fast silence. The atmosphere was charged with gloom, despair, sorrow—and death.

Death, alas, was the next thing that something had to be done about. Nearly a third of the town's inhabitants had died and they all had to be buried. The stench of scorched flesh and necrosis already filled the nostrils of the living. Martinius Rheinbeck, with all the persuasion and gentleness at his command, persuaded the relatives and friends of the dead that a mass grave was the only possible solution to such a tragic problem. There were only two shovels and it would take far too long to bury each corpse individually, and the vultures would be coming soon enough and would literally have to be fought off if the task took all night as it certainly would. Too, the single grave would serve as a shrine for what the town had meant and could have been to all these good people. Pilgrimages could be made to it in the future, and God in his wisdom would understand and no one would blame anyone in the town for agreeing to such a thing. It was practical; it was sensible—it was Christian. In the end, despite the loud laments of some widows, the thing was done. With all the men taking turns on the only shovels. Toward midnight the grave was deep enough to accommodate all, each cadaver being laid gently to rest, side by side, arms folded across chest, facing the dark heavens. There were stars again that night, and a moon still full. Martinius Rheinbeck stood with his book at the massive end of the grave and intoned solemnly: "*I am the Resurrection and the Light.*"

David Bard joined with all the men in shoveling mounds of earth down upon the immobile faces. The shovels, hands, feet—all were used to cover up the massed dead ones. When it was at last done, the moon had hidden behind a cloud. And the stars lost some of their brightness. A great hush fell over the assembled mourners. It was as if they would not go away unless Martinius Rheinbeck told them to. He did in a great, gentle voice, as a father would talk to a child.

"And now to bed. Get some rest. There is no more we can do this night. In the morning the Lord, in his infinite wisdom and mercy, will show us the path out of this dark and evil time. God bless you all, and I commend you to the care of the Almighty."

After all that had happened, there was nothing for anyone to do but try to get some sleep, as a surcease from sorrow, as a shutting off of the mind from the terrible calamity that had struck that day. In the wilderness and desolation left, the threescore survivors found burrows and folds in the earth and shut their eyes. Silence fell over the area. Even the whimpering children at last succumbed to utter exhaustion. Martinius Rheinbeck, Sister Edna Sunset and David Bard, the visitors in Horsefall, remained with the Conestoga wagon on the perimeter of the sleeping, huddled figures. All the campfires had burned low.

David Bard, try as he might, could not sleep. His mind was too troubled, too confused by all that had happened. So he crawled quietly from underneath the wagon and carefully made his way in the darkness toward a big rock which gleamed slablike in the light of the waning moon. It was some sixty yards distant from the makeshift camp and would be an ideal spot to sit by himself and reflect on what was and what was to be.

The rock stood like a landmark, a dividing line between the thick forest and what had been Horsefall. David reached it and was preparing to sit back against its sloping front when, to his great surprise, he realized he wasn't alone. Someone else had also chosen the rock for solitude. From the other side of the rocky mound, a soft voice murmured, "I am here, too, David."

It was Sister Edna Sunset, speaking in a low hush, her tone very quiet and sad. David joined her, his heart and all his senses suddenly tom-tomming like Indian drums. With the huge rock behind them, they were shut off from the view of all the sleeping townspeople. And it was a time, an interlude, that was all at once unbearably intimate and very special indeed. The moon, the stars, the stillness, were all of a piece.

David Bard sat by her side. Their shoulders touched, but she did not look at him. The shawl covering her shoulders hid her hands. Her face was to him in profile, almost silhouetted against the night. He could not see the gold of her hair nor the blue of her eyes, but he remembered all too well.

"I could not sleep, David."

"Me neither."

"It was so terrible today—the women, the children; all those dead people—this morning they were alive."

"I know, I know."

"It all came back to me out there while Martinius was doing his good work—God's work—my mother and father; Cooperstown, the Mohawk Valley; the slaughter . . ."

"Don't, Edna, please. That don't do no good."

"I want to talk about it now. I must. I have never spoken about it to anyone. Not even Martinius."

"Edna—"

"There are some things a body can't tell some folks, but you're different—you're like me; we're both orphans. . . ."

He found her cold hands under the concealing shawl. He clasped them warmly, squeezing them. He knew he would not be able to still her tongue, that she suddenly felt a great need to unburden herself to him. Inwardly he exulted. He was glad. She had remained aloof from him since the moment he had stumbled bleeding from the woods. But now—now, she was drawing close to him, speaking low, her very tone suggesting trust, liking, and best of all, confidence in him as a man not to betray her weakness. He swallowed, his mouth dry again, as it always seemed to be when he was anywhere near Sister Edna Sunset.

So he listened as she spoke on.

It was not a pretty story, as familiar as it was. The Indian-white man troubles never were. This was a particularly grim and savage tale. And in the end, it ended as most of them usually did. With the Hurons on a rampage, sweeping through Cooperstown and killing and butchering. Sister Edna had seen her parents tomahawked and scalped and she had not been able to do anything to save them. She had lain terrified, stunned, beneath a fallen tree, hiding herself from the depradating braves running amok through the village. Sister Edna Sunset suddenly inclined her head and now it rested on David Bard's broad shoulder. She said no more, but he was aware of her fragrance— like honey and sweet flowers—and his own heart was beating so loudly he was certain she could hear it.

She was so silent, waiting, that he knew it was his turn to tell a tale of early orphanhood. So he quietly and unhurriedly told of the senseless death of Michael Winship Bard at the hands of a drunken soldier. And the earlier loss of Frances Hepburn Bard in an unlucky child-birthing. Sister

Edna Sunset moaned at the conclusion of his own sad story. A low moan, not of pain, but of pure uncomprehension. "Oh, David . . ."

"It's all past, Edna. No use fretting."

"I know, I know. But the Lord confuses me sometimes—the people he sees fit to take and the ones he sees fit to leave here on earth."

For a moment he forgot her and the rising tide of passion in his chest. "Ain't that the truth? Like those bastards yesterday with that poor black fellow—God damn them!"

"Don't be profane, David."

He squeezed her hands again, which were no longer cold.

"All right, Edna. If you say so."

"I do say so."

"Now you sould like Martinius. You know that?"

Her face turned toward him. She was close now. All too close. He could almost see her blue eyes in the shadows. Suddenly, without a conscious, willful thought, he brushed his lips against hers. For one second she recoiled. And then she did not. Her lips pressed up at him. Urgently, almost questioningly. She kept her hands underneath the shawl and he did not make the mistake of seizing her roughly. Only their lips touched and—it was like something he had never known. But it was also like exactly what he had fancied so many times it would be these last few days. Her mouth was making him drunk. The blood roared within him; his heart soared.

She drew back, but she did not take her face away.

"David . . ." His name was the barest whisper in the

stillness of the night. And never had it sounded more lyrical.

"Yes?"

"I have never kissed a man before—not since I have been a woman grown."

"Edna, you don't have to—"

"Hush—please let me say what I have to say, for we will never talk of this again—I have never kissed a man because I have never wanted to. Do you understand? I felt no need, no desire—maybe that is why it was easy for me to embrace God and go with Martinius, but I don't feel . . . that way . . . now . . ."

He blinked in the darkness, as if his ears were deceiving him or he hadn't heard right. "You telling me, Edna, that you—"

"Yes, David—I have wanted that kiss from you since I first . . . saw your goodness. You are also a beautiful person to look at—and I—inside me I felt stirrings and feelings I have never had before . . . feelings I don't understand . . . even now, sitting like this with you, I'm all on fire . . . like something was eating me up inside. Oh, David . . ." Her voice had risen now, almost desperate, and he could wait no longer. His hunger for her, his mounting warmth, completely overwhelmed all his good intentions. His arms went around her and he drew the tall, full body to him, his mouth burning down on hers in the darkness. She did not resist. Their lips fused in a molten union. And then he was kissing her lips, her eyes, her nose, her brow, murmuring her name over and over again in a kind of dazed litany. And unbelievably, she was saying his name in the same wonder-filled tones. "David . . . David . . . my David . . ."

"Edna—by God—I love you!" It seemed to cannon from his soul.

She said nothing to that, but she pushed him away gently and put her head to his chest, not looking at him anymore. Her voice came to him as if from some faraway shore. Like an echo. Very low, and amazingly calm and sweet.

"I have never been with anyone, David. . . . I don't think I would even know what to do . . . but you must be patient with me . . . and kind. I cannot do what every ounce of me wants to do this very second. Please, understand . . . David. I would not be able to look Martinius in the face in the morning."

"By God," he exclaimed heatedly. "That don't matter! Honest, Edna. As long as you love me—really do, I mean—I can wait. We both can wait."

"You are sweet, David—very sweet—and God bless you, my love."

The moon shone down and the handful of stars glittered magically. David Bard and Edna Sunset kissed again. And again. Until they could bear the kisses no longer and she abruptly gathered up her skirts and fled to the safety of the Conestoga, disappearing into the moonlit gloom like a wraith.

David Bard leaned his back against the big rock and stared up at the heavens. Joy throbbed throughout his entire being. And all thoughts of misery, gloom, despair, and his association with John Brown vanished from his heart and soul forever. He knew his way now, was certain of his path. His destiny. No matter what happened tomorrow or the next day he was bound to Martinius Rheinbeck until the day of kingdom come. And all the time thereafter.

Martinius Rheinbeck and . . .

Sister Edna Sunset.

Glory, glory, hallelujah!

The moments spent with her, the utter intimacy, the sharing, the love mutually declared, all that had contrived to make David Bard feel ten feet tall. Like the millions of men before him, and the millions to come, he had partaken of that particular and specific phenomenon that had occurred in the Garden of Eden between Adam and Eve. The first man and the first woman, according to Scripture. And all the available authorities on the subject of the creation. And mankind's beginning.

So on that awful day in obliterated Horsefall, another man and another woman felt and experienced that emotion which inevitably leads to the turning of the world.

David Bard and Edna Sunset slept apart from one another with their hearts full of love and their heads in the clouds.

They could not have dared dream or even suspect the thorny, hazardous road on which that love was to take them.

The road to damnation was indeed paved with good intentions. And salvation was to prove powerfully hard to attain.

As the Devil only knew.

BOOK TWO

EXODUS:
DAVID BARD, PRODIGAL
SON

BIBLES AND BULLETS

If David Bard had thought Martinius Rheinbeck a leader and organizer of all things before, that was as nothing compared to the manner in which he took the devastated townspeople of Horsefall in tow the next day. No leader of any flock, no Moses leading his people out of Egypt, could have done better. David looked on in awe and marveled anew, all the while keeping his eyes on Sister Edna Sunset and their new, almost frighteningly sweet secret. She deliberately kept away from him during Martinius' reorganization of what was left of a burned-out town. Sister Edna was far too occupied helping the womenfolk seeing to the children and the cooking and the washing of wounds and so many other things. But above and beyond all that was the tower of strength in the black suit and the high, wide-brimmed hat. David helped, of course, as was his duty, but somehow he felt the incredible preacher-man could have done it all without him. It was a fine lesson in perseverance, strength, and faith. David's admiration for the man grew yet larger and firmer. Martinius Rheinbeck was father, counselor, preacher, doctor, the law, and kindness, all in one man.

First, he called for the leaders of Horsefall, if yet alive, those men who had been the fathers of the growing settlement. These proved to be three very diverse individuals called Richard Clear, Rusty Hevelin, and Andy Beigel. Soon they gathered at the Conestoga for a conference as the rest of the survivors went about the ruins, still searching, not yet fully convinced that all was indeed lost. Clear, Hevelin, and Beigel had been three men who had more or less been appointed by their neighbors to set the town on its feet. Clear had been selected as a mayor of sorts; Hevelin had served in the capacity of a judge to study all grievances and pass judgment on them. Beigel's task had been the supplies and provisions to make certain Horsefall would not suffer from lack of food and water until the town got on its feet and was able to provide for all. Martinius Rheinbeck spoke to them as a group, for he had much to say. And in the saying and the remarks elicited from the three men in response, he was much impressed with the calibre of Horsefall's leaders. David Bard sat in on the powwow, for all things that involved Rheinbeck involved him and Sister Edna Sunset. They were a family now.

Clear and Hevelin both were in their middle years, businessmen who had sold out their bookstores in Dayton, Ohio, to try a new land and a fresh life. But now their chagrin about yesterday was giving way to new hope as Rheinbeck talked on. Clear was a stocky man of solid proportions whose hairless face held rather intense darkly brown eyes. But his voice was soft and accented with Ohio echoes. Hevelin was a paradox. He wore a wide, flowing beard and his long hair hung to his shoulders, like any frontiersman, but the craftiness of his face was belied by a resonant voice that carried across a room with easy power and human friendliness. Andy Beigel, the oldest of the three, was a slight, wiry man whose perpetually sad expression had nothing to do with the highly elevated heel of his right shoe, a device that compensated for a dragging left leg. Beigel was a retired railroad man who had come from New Jersey to try his luck in Horsefall with the new settlers. Beigel's sadness was thoroughly a characteristic of his face and had little to do with a warm and generous nature. All these conclusions Martinius Rheinbeck made on the spot, and David Bard saw and heard the corroboration of them as the four men had their conference. It was educational.

"Then it's your thinking, Preacher," Richard Clear said very slowly in his soft, easy voice, "that we stay and see this thing through?"

"The Lord will provide," Rheinbeck smiled, "if you show him you have the gumption and the determination to fight difficulties and hardships."

Rusty Hevelin fingers his Santa Claus-like beard whose redness was like that of carrots and brick. "I'm all for that, but it's kind of dismal-looking right now, wouldn't you all say?"

Andy Beigel winked and the sadness of his dourly lean face vanished in a twinkling. "When we lost a train, we put another one right back on the line. No sense in standing still and counting what we lost. Let's see what we can do all over again."

Martinius Rheinbeck beamed on him with full approval.

"Well put, Brother Beigel. I can see to the souls and spiritual salvation of your people, gentlemen, but it is up to you to guide them in the practical matters of everyday existence here and now, in the hour of their greatest trial."

Richard Clear nodded. "I know what you mean. Fancy talk won't do it. We need food, water, shelter—we don't get them, then we all better start walking back to where we came from. Heck, we haven't got horses, rigs—not even a plough or a furrow anymore. That damn fire—" He broke off, stopping himself from a blasphemy on the Ritter family and their mischievous dog and child. Rusty Hevelin put a consoling arm on his shoulder. "Just when we were seeing some daylight in all the problems that go with a new town. Why, we were fixing to build a church for you, Preacher—"

"Time enough for that later, Mr. Clear. No, now this is what we must do. Food—that is of immediate importance. David Bard there will take the shotguns we have and you will assign your best shot to help him. There is a running stream not far from here. Assign a detail of men to take the barrels from my wagon. The water we can boil. As for shelter, the forests nearby will provide enough wood for two towns—if there are men willing to spit on their hands and do the proper job. All these things can be done—until your people see daylight again, as you say so aptly." Martinius Rheinbeck paused, his dark brown eyes passing from face to face of the men before him. "I have a crate of Bibles in the wagon. David will open that and pass them out to your people. The word of the Lord is of great help to those who have suffered."

Rusty Hevelin coughed apologetically.

"Hold on, now. There aren't that many who can read among us. All good people, Preacher, mind you, but book-learning is something a lot of them have no knack at all for."

"It is of no matter. The Book and its presence will be a comfort to them. I will guide them in the ways and meanings of the word come next Sunday at our service out in the open. You will see. Those of you who can read will be my spiritual assistants."

David Bard, who could read, for he had not let the tragedy of his parents' deaths stop him—Ma and Pa had been great for keeping after him to do so, besides—suddenly felt a need to horn in on the conversation. "Excuse me, Martinius, but I'm good with books and words—I could help some of the older boys."

Rheinbeck abruptly chuckled and everyone looked at him in surprise, most of all David Bard, for he had never heard the preacher so amused. "What's funny about that, Martinius?"

"Forgive me, my good boy. Yes, I know you can read. You also have a fine voice with timbre and clarity. But I yet must teach you to dismiss certain unfortunate words from your vocabulary that tend to make you sound like you cannot read at all."

"Such as?" David was genuinely puzzled.

"Such as words like *ain't* and *sure*—and a few others. But no matter. You will outgrow such words the longer you stay with myself and the Lord. I will see to that. I have you marked for great things, David. You must not disappoint me. Your voice is perfect for Gospel."

There was such feeling and intensity in this last that David could only nod, swallow hard, and suddenly pay attention to the butt of the Navy Colt strapped to his hip. Andy Beigel came to his rescue.

"Here now, we got a passel of folks who can read in our settlement. There's Frank Hamilton, Walter Miller, Don Higgins, Al Tonik, Bob Sampson; and some of the women, too—Di Sampson, for one. And what about Amy Highland—she even went to school in New York—that so, Richard?"

"That's right," Clear agreed with jubilation. "Why, that settles that all around, I think. Rusty?"

Hevelin's crafty eyes gleamed. "That's the least of the problem. Like the Preacher said—survival comes first."

"Then let's about it," Martinius Rheinbeck declared, "before this fine day grows an hour older. With the help of you gentlemen, I know in my heart, Horsefall will rise from the ashes again like the phoenix. There are towns close enough to reach—they will help with supplies, tools, as soon as we are able to convey our great need to them."

"Horsefall," grunted Rusty Hevelin. "Never did like that name. Best we find a new one, huh, Richard?"

"It's worth thinking about," Richard Clear said.

Andy Beigel snorted. "Blasted name was a jinx right from the start—felt it in my old bones—a horse falling sure isn't any kind of good luck."

"Time enough later for that," Martinius Rheinbeck intoned very sternly. "Now, gentlemen, let us concern ourselves with the immediate. And the necessary. Jehovah will see to the rest."

"Amen to that," David Bard muttered feelingly, without a conscious memory that he had spoken his thoughts out loud.

The conclave broke up and every man set about to do

the things that staying alive and keeping a large amount of people safe and sound called for. The nearby town of Whitney could be alerted for help. No one knew it then, but the settlement of Horsefall had truly ceased to exist from that moment on.

And it wasn't because of the destructive conflagration which had eaten the town into nothingness. And oblivion.

It was the death of the name *Horsefall*.

A curious cognomen which would never be used again.

The powers-that-were-and-would-be-again, Richard Clear, Rusty Hevelin, and Andy Beigel, would have their way—and their say—ultimately. Horsefall was no more.

And the phoenix was stirring in the black and charred ashes.

When they had gone, David shook himself into action.

"Well, I'd better see to the shotguns and do something about getting this town some food—" He broke off, for Martinius Rheinbeck was not listening. "You feeling all right, Martinius?"

The older man stirred, as if coming out of some deep trance. He looked at his young follower with unspoken affection.

"I am sorry, David. It was just that I was remembering my Scripture—a quotation that has often kept my spirits up in times of stress and fear." The dark eyes took on light. "*The Lord is my strength and my song.*"

"You quoting just then, Martinius?"

"Yes, David. I was quoting. From one of the books of the Bible. Exodus: Chapter Fifteen, Verse Two."

David Bard's smile was truly a glowing one.

"My Ma told me a fine one once. Never did forget it.

She was a lot like you, Martinius Rheinbeck. She believed all her life in the Bible and the power of goodness.''

"I should like to have known her, David. Would you speak the quotation for me now? Please.''

"Sure—I mean, yes.'' David's grin was sheepish, but he lost the grin when he repeated softly the words that Frances Hepburn Bard had spoken many times over him as he lay abed: "*Better to light one candle than to curse the darkness.*''

Martinius Rheinbeck's eyes glittered with feeling.

"St. Christopher—of course. The patron saint of ferry-men and travelers—aye. We will abide by that advice this day. And from this day hence.''

"I'd venture you been doing that right along, Martinius.''

For a long moment, the preacher did not speak. And then he said: "David, I will now say to you what you once said to me but yesterday—I am that proud to know you. Now go and do as I bid you. There has been enough talk.''

And so there had.

Yet when David Bard took his leave from Martinius Rheinbeck to fetch the shotguns and meet whoever had been designated by the leaders to assist him in hunting game, he left with the feeling, not faint at all, that the preacher had been sorrowful, in spite of all his optimistic talk. It was a curious notion to have about Martinius Rheinbeck and David did not like it. Not one bit.

All unaware, David Bard had had a premonition of danger.

Of death. A sensation of something bad about to happen.

One he was to remember before this long day was done.

The shadow of the beyond had stretched its fearful shadow across the curved length of the Conestoga wagon

and the tall black-suited figure of Martinius Rheinbeck.
The man of God.

Though the sun was bright in the sky and a fleet of
white clouds scudded like schooners in nautical formation.

Death yet hovered over the site of the town that had
been Horsefall. Death who would not take his holiday, not
just yet.

Not when there was more killing to be done.

And more dying.

He saw Sister Edna Sunset before he shoved off into the
woods with a young man called Link Hullar. Richard
Clear had told him that Hullar was the best shot in town.
David Bard saw no reason to disagree with him, but while
the mild-mannered youth in the ragged, smoked-out garb
waited for him, he stopped for a word with Sister Edna.
She had had her hands full all morning, and when he saw
her, a smudge of flour stained her smooth cheek and the
long, golden hair hung damply. Her sleeves were rolled up
and her tawny arms showed soot and dust. But the
cornflower-blue eyes still held the softness he remembered
from last night.

"Will you be gone long, David?"

"Be back just as soon as me and the sharpshooter bag
some fowl. Maybe a deer—these woods should be full of
them."

"Just you be careful."

"I will. I got a lot to keep me wanting to stay
alive—now."

There was no more to be said. The look in her eyes told
him what he wanted to know. The magic of last night yet
remained.

Whistling now, he joined Link Hullar who was waiting for him, idly checking the other shotgun. Hullar had to be a few years older, but he did not look it. His face was the kind that seemed like it would never grow any hair, though his dark brown locks were full and neatly in place, framing his pleasant face.

"Shotguns ain't—aren't—much," David grinned, "for bringing down birds and they'll spoil four-legged game some, but we'll have to make them do. This camp needs food."

"We won't come back empty-handed, Bard. If there's anything out there, we'll get them," Link Hullar declared without conceit. "I was the best shot in Brockton. Won a turkey shoot when I was no more'n fourteen."

"Brockton?"

"Massachusetts. That's where I come from when I joined up with Clear and Hevelin and this drive to set up a new town. Shame it ain't gonna be—"

"We better see some turkeys then," David laughed, ignoring the sad remark. These people would have to keep their spirits up, like Martinius wanted them to. "And I'll show you some shooting, too. I once hit a hawk bucking in a stiff breeze."

"You're on," Hullar said grimly. "See who bags the most."

With that youthful bravado they both struck off for the distant woods. The day was mild enough and there was little wind. October had proven a pretty fair month for weather.

Behind them, the survivors were all going about the business of survival and picking up the pieces of yesterday's holocaust. It was not easy to do. Three more people had died overnight—elderly pioneers who had succumbed to their bad burns, burns which normally would not have proven fatal, with proper medical attention, but the aftermath of shock and horror had added to the death toll of Horsefall. The funeral detail would be busy once more, but this time separate, individual graves would be dug.

"When we get back, Hullar," David suddenly remembered something, "I got to open a crate of Bibles. I'd be much obliged if you helped me pass them out to your people."

"Be glad to, Bard."

Twenty minutes later, as they stalked quietly in the still forest, eyes alert, senses quickened, they had become David and Link. The young never stood on ceremony very long, especially when shoulder-to-shoulder in hard times. And emergencies.

But Death walked with them.

Death who was no stranger to the settlement that had been known as Horsefall.

The clouds of black smoke which had shrouded the horizon the day before had done more than signal the end of Horsefall; it had served as a beacon, a message, to those who would profit from disaster. Like an invitation in the sky, the roiling signs of the town's demise had been seen from miles away. Not by fellow settlers or other white men, no. But by a renegade band of Fox Indians who had long since quite the formal life of their tribe, refusing to be a part of a community. Wild young bucks, twenty in all, who had roved the countryside, living off the land and existing by their wits and sheer savagery. They had looted lonely cabins in the wilderness, plundered from passing wagon trains, and murdered all "white eyes" that they encountered. More than one scalp dangled from their counting sticks—the long pole taken into battle with which the brave would touch a rider-enemy and then depart, boasting of his accomplishments to the tribe. But these bucks went beyond touching. They killed and scalped and butchered anyone who fell into their brutal hands.

They had forsaken their teepees and wickiups; they lived in the forest, the cold ground their beds. They were two-feather Indians—no war bonnets for these men, for none of them were chiefs. All of them were young, ruthless, and unskilled in red man practicalities such as making mocassins and stripping the bark off trees to make maps and necessary accessories. In truth, this wild band of young savages knew only the law of the bow and arrow and the rifles and pistols they had captured from their fallen victims.

It was this vicious crew of Fox warriors, all of them mounted on saddleless paint ponies, who saw the rising cloud of black smoke climbing in the western sky. They understood and they smiled to each other, their eyes gleaming with avarice and cruelty. Black smoke meant fire; fire meant destruction—the white man was in trouble of some kind. The Fox braves danced and chanted before they rode off in the direction of the telltale cloud of smoke.

Each of them was a superb horseman. All of them had ridden since they were old enough to walk. The twenty horses galloped in single-file formation, threading one perilous path through the tall pines and the dense foliage of the forest. Surely and expertly.

There was no singing now. No savage war whoops.

That would come later.

When they reached the place where the smoke came from.

But all of their eyes flicked in anticipation.

A raid on whites meant more guns, more food, women, and perhaps firewater—which red men could not handle but liked enormously because it made them feel so light-headed.

The Fox braves moved on quickly. Urging their ponies.

What had happened to Horsefall only yesterday was as nothing now, compared to what was coming.

And what was to be.

Like the benighted John Brown, these renegade bucks were going on a raid. A lightninglike surprise attack.

But not to capture, take, and hold.

Only to kill.

There was a difference.

THE LAST STAND

They had bagged about six rabbits, two turkeys, and one large deer when David Bard called a halt to the hunt. Now there was the problem of getting the kills back to camp. Link Hullar had been every bit as good a shot as he had said he was. The deer and two rabbits were his. While a shotgun and a Navy Colt were not exactly the proper weapons for bringing down game, for the blasts would spoil the better part of the meat, both young men had executed fine head shots. All in all, the kill total was a fair one for but two hours' work.

David looped the rabbits and turkeys into one trussed heap, using his buckskin jacket as a carrying sack. He knotted the sleeves together making for a compact bundle.

"Think you can handle this, Link?" He indicated the bound load of bird and animal. "I'll tote the deer across my shoulders. Shouldn't be too much for me."

"Reckon I can. They're sure gonna be happy when we show up with all this food, David."

"Amen to that."

They had roved and searched more than a mile from camp. So they began the return journey, following the same route they had come. Through the trees, over rising hillocks of earth, across clearings and back into the forest again. The cool air had made their strenuous efforts less arduous than they would have been on a hot day. The pale sun seemed to keep pace with them as they hefted their loads. When they paused for a necessary stop to rest themselves and uncramp their tired arms and legs, they were only a mere thousand yards from the spot where a town called Horsefall had tried to erect a settlement in the wilderness. Link Hullar dropped to the green earth for a breather. His hairless face was flushed with exertion and excitement. David had allowed his own stubble to grow, never having asked Martinius for his razor. A fine one inch growth bordered his lean chin and jaws—something that Sister Edna had never mentioned last night.

"Sure wish I had a tobacco chaw," Link sighed.

"Be glad you haven't. Ma always said it was bad for the teeth. I kinda went along with that. Pa did too."

"Well, it seems to me," Link Hullar was about to disagree, "that a man needs something to—"

It was then that the shots came to them.

The sound of them. Staccato, one right after the other, and then the most unusual cries they had ever heard. Like the yelping of a pack of dogs or a bunch of banshees screaming in the night. For one long hard moment both young men looked at each other. Then came the shots again. A thumping and pounding of rifle fire that sounded like somebody beating on a drum. The sudden uproar, as faint and as distant as it was, was unmistakable. And readily identifiable.

"That's Horsefall!" Link Hullar blurted, rising to his feet.

"That's Indians!" David Bard shouted, the heart within his buckskin shirt sinking like the sun did in the west everyday. When there was a sun. All those poor defenseless people back there, and Martinius Rheinbeck, and Sister Edna Sunset—Edna—his Edna *Oh, Lord, help us now*. There had hardly been any weapons in camp at all—nothing to fight back with except the handguns the men still had on their hips—Clear, Hevelin, Beigel, and some of the other—but all those women and children!

They forgot all about their game loads.

They ran across the clearing, tearing through the forest that separated them from the burned-out patch of ground where they had left all their friends and relatives. And those they loved.

Even as they drew closer, the sounds of firing and yelling, and now the fierce terror of women screaming, rose in volume and intensity. The terrible screams made their blood freeze in their veins.

David Bard pushed ugly pictures and horrible images from his wildly unreasoning mind as he and Link Hullar hurtled toward camp. And the Lord alone knew what.

It was like the end of the world, again.

No United States cavalryman or trick rider could have matched what the band of Fox braves did that awesome afternoon. Once they had scouted the target, grunting their disappointment in so much ruin and wreckage with little left to see worth looting, they had remounted their paint ponies, taken what high ground there was, and then come sweeping down in an all-out attack worthy of any military man with general's stars on his shoulders. There had been but fifty souls left of the original population, thanks to the deadly fire and the deaths from injuries sustained, but the Fox braves had seen enough palefaced women to merit their time and effort. The white man's squaws, easily recognizable by their long hair and those bell-shaped things they wore called dresses. And skirts. Women were always a prize for Indians on a raid. To serve, to cook, to pleasure a brave. Also, they could be used in barter and trade with other red men. For guns, food, clothing, and even firewater. The children would be worthless unless there were truly fine specimens among the catch. All men would be killed. It was the Indian code of survival. Too, one gained wisdom and strength and the blessing of the gods when one killed a white man.

So the renegade band thundered down on what remained of Horsefall. Catching every soul in camp flat-footed and helpless.

They came in a wide, sweeping arc, their lithe bodies low to the sides of their mounts, presenting no target at all. And each of them so skilled with the bow and arrow that slaughter was almost immediate. In the first swoop, a flight of arrows winged across the flat ground and nearly every one of them found a target. Men, women, and children went down, their hands still busy with the chores that had been allotted to them that day by the town's fathers. The Fox band wheeled, turned in a graceful circle and came pounding back for another pass. Now the braves who had rifles brought these into play. Their fire-sticks cracked and boomed. It was then and only then that the men of the town responded to the initial assault. They fell to the ground, finding cover behind every bit of wreckage they could and fired furiously.

Martinius Rheinbeck, his Bible still in his bronzed fingers, looked up in dumbfounded amazement from the platform of the Conestoga wagon. Sister Edna Sunset, no more than twenty feet away, carrying a bucket of water, was between him and the rampaging Fox Indians. With a mighty oath, Rheinbeck leaped from the wagon and stalked toward the attackers, holding up his long arms, beseeching them to stop their mad attack. From their cover nearby, on the hard earth, Richard Clear and Rusty Hevelin shouted to him to get down, even as they blasted away with their pistols as the horses of the Foxes raised clouds of dust. But Martinius Rheinbeck kept on walking, his dark brown eyes almost raised to the heavens as he called on the Lord to put an end to this senseless slaughter. But no one was listening to him.

Two riderless horses came racing around the wagon, proof that some of Horsefall's bullets had found their mark. Sister Edna had dropped her waterbucket and was running toward the tall figure of Rheinbeck, calling out to him to come back. Clear and Hevelin exchanged pitying looks and then proceeded to flank both the preacher and his woman with covering fire. Andy Beigel, in the heart of the camp, pressed behind a tree stump, a tree that had been cut down but a week ago, was using an old muzzle-loader with telling effect. A gun he had rescued from the disaster of the day before. Three more braves bit the dust, but the toll on Horsefall's side was devastating. All about Beigel, the dead and dying lay, with arrows sticking from their chests and backs. Some of them were children.

The air was still filled with high, fierce shouts in Indian language. There were but a dozen braves left, but one more unified sweep across the remaining defenders of Horsefall and it might be sufficient to carry the day.

All those alive, huddling fearfully on the scorched earth, would never forget the events of the next few minutes. It was to become a legend. A tall story, a tale told around campfires for years to come. The sort of thing that no one could every really believe, as grand as it was to hear. But to those who remained alive in the town that had been Horsefall, it was gospel. The holy truth.

And it happened right before their eyes.

The twelve marauding Indians began to dissolve. One by one. In all the melee and the screaming and the dusty confusion, no one could say for sure what was happening. But a brave toppled from a pony, and then another and another. Horses reared and kicked; the Foxes continued to shoot their arrows and their guns. But suddenly it was apparent to all that but six braves remained on horseback. All the others lay on the hard, bloodstained earth, as dead as doornails. And finally the mounted braves wheeled and saw the thing that was undoing them. Two more white eyes, silhouetted on the rising mound of earth off to their left. Two more guns, a long-barreled fire-stick and a pistol. The sun gleamed off the revolver. A Navy Colt.

With a fierce cry of rage, the nominal leader of the band cried out in his native tongue, and the remainder of the party all abruptly rode back the way they had come, pounding through the mass of dead bodies. And still the guns smoked from the hillock of earth, and two more dark-skinned savages were flung from their horses, shot dead-center in their brown backs. The dazed people of Horsefall lurched to their feet, witness to a miracle. They were saved again—the hand of the Lord, or just two sharpshooters who knew their business.

But it was not to end there. Not just yet.

Martinius Rheinbeck, dazed, dusty, his exhortations completely ignored, miraculously untouched by bullet or arrow in his foolhardy role of peacemaker, continued to run after the retreating redskins. His mighty arms pumped into the air. His powerful bass voice rose in a thunderous blast of words. "GO, YOU HEATHEN DEVILS, YOU CANNOT TAKE AWAY THE CHILDREN OF THE LORD!"

And then the last rider, pounding out of the scorched-town that had seemed such an easy mark for an enterprising band of renegades, turned on his pony and let fly one last arrow. An avenging arrow.

A feathered destroyer which sang across the clearing. And thudded directly into the broad chest of Martinius Rheinbeck. An impossible shot but a true one. The tip of the arrow had pierced Martinius Rheinbeck's heart. Pinning the black frock coat to the broad chest.

In a stunned silence, made more loud by the sudden cessation of gunfire and war whoops as the Fox braves disappeared back over the ridge, all eyes were on the preacher. All hearts stopped.

The tall figure stood stock-still for but a moment. Motionless.

Then the eyes, the piercing dark brown beacons of hope and love, closed forever. The black-suited form fell. Face-forward in the bloody dust, it quivered, and did not move again. A low universal moan went up, from all those who still had the eyes to see the calamity. And rue it.

Richard Clear cursed; Rusty Hevelin spat tobacco with meaningful finality on the hard earth. Andy Beigel let his muzzle-loader slip from his fingers, his bitter face more dour than ever.

The only ones who did not see Martinius Rheinbeck fall were David Bard and Link Hullar, slumping down from the high ground where they had stationed themselves with maximum results. Hullar had proven himself a dead shot. The turkey shoot at Brockton had been no myth. David Bard had thanked God there was enough ammunition for the Colt revolver. He had put it to better use than Pete Tarzy ever did.

But . . .

Sister Edna Sunset was on her knees, hands clasped in prayer, eyes filled with tears, over someone lying in the dust. A long man in a black suit—there was a book lying nearby. A Bible, its brown leather cover stained with something red—fresh blood.

With the shock that comes with awful recognition, David Bard could not speak. His brain had ceased to function. As well as his heart and soul. Martinius dead? *It couldn't be!*

One look at Sister Edna Sunset's blood-drained sweet face told him otherwise. The mighty fall from time to time, and this time a truly great one had settled into the dust. Never to rise again.

Not in this world, at any rate.

Hopefully in the next if there was any God at all.

Or justice.

Heedless, moved by some force within him, David Bard

fell to his knees beside the still figure and buried his face on the dead chest before him. A great sorrow, a terrible hurt, unbidden, welled up within him and suddenly, "Oh, God . . ." The words pushed from in a wrenching sob. "Why . . . *why?* . . . Martinius. . . ."

There was no reply from the inert form in his arms. There could not be. A heavy silence hung over the scene. No one spoke; no one moved. The sun looked down on a tableau of numerous figures that might have been painted. Statuelike, all who remained alive in Horsefall looked on mutely as a young man gave in to a tremendous, over-whelming loss which had swiftly come home to him—unexpectedly, flashingly, like a summer storm breaking over the prairies.

The dead bodies strewn across the blasted landscape, white man and red man alike, were but another sad mosaic of man's inhumanity to man. And overhead a lazy flight of vultures circled slowly, warily, in the peaceful blue sky. Buzzards who could wait, their bald, beaked heads uglier than ever, were all too familiar. The vultures did not cry out, making no sound at all save for the soft whirring of their black wings. They knew better. The carrion below would not go away. Not just yet.

Soft hands touched David Bard's heaving shoulders. The melodious voice, bent to his ear, whispered tenderly: "David, David . . . come away . . . he is with the Lord now. . . ."

He shook himself, not turning, still clasping Martinius Rheinbeck's big, bronzed right hand. "Why . . . Edna . . . why him? . . . he was so good . . . so. . . ." He could not finish. He was a child again, a tearful, heartbro-ken boy crouching over the fallen form of Michael Winship

Bard, dead from a mad drunken soldier's bullet. *Pa . . . Martinius . . . Ma . . .* The tears would not stop. They cascaded from his eyes and he did not care, did not think that he was as a child in front of the others. In front of Sister Edna Sunset.

"Be strong, David."

She spoke quietly so that no one else could hear.

"Edna, I . . ."

"You must carry on for him now, David. You must do his work. I will help you. Together we will be what Martinius Rheinbeck died for. Hear me well, David Bard. From this moment on, it is your sworn duty and mine. Do you hear me, David Bard? I love you."

"I hear you."

"Then stand up. Take me by the hand. Turn and face these people. They will look to us for guidance—that is the way it will have to be. He would want us to stand together for him."

He stood up then, brushing angrily at his eyes. He pulled his glazed view away from the familiar bearded face beneath him and straightened his back. When he at last faced the grim onlookers who had waited for him to speak, he was no longer crying. His young features had hardened, tightened into a mold of determination and self-control. Only his eyes betrayed him. But his voice did not when he lifted it and almost hurled it at them all. Not angrily, but with full power and make-no-mistake-about-it authority.

"Martinius Rheinbeck is dead, God bless him. We will bury him in a separate grave up there by that grassy hillock. No man will speak words over him but me. As I will for all the others who fell this day." He reached down and slowly picked up the bloodstained Bible from the dusty earth. He held it tightly in his hands and almost felt a flow of some kind of strange strength from the buckram leather cover with the cross printed on its surface. The Christian crucifix, the Holy Cross. For a long moment he silently prayed. Then at last he said: "I am your new preacher. And I will speak for Martinius Rheinbeck. And the Good Lord."

David Bard was not prepared for what happened on the heels of this announcement. Nor was Sister Edna Sunset. These people who had suffered so much, lost so much, who had had their world turned upside down, now responded in a manner that was nothing less than miraculous and breathtaking. And totally marvelous.

A great cheer went up, a rising chorus of *Hallelujah!* and *Glory be to God!* and *The Lord bless you, David Bard!* The women wept openly; the men poked at their eyes—and even in the midst of all that loss, carnage, and death, humanity spoke up. In a loud, clear, voice. The Devil take the hindmost! The Good Book would prevail.

Richard Clear smiled happily, his benevolent face calm once more. Rusty Hevelin bit off another plug of tobacco with vehement enthusiasm. Andy Beigel raised his muzzle-loader over his dour head and pumped enthusiastically. Link Hullar, grimy young face awash with excitement, put his hands together and shook them in congratulations and admiration for his new friend David Bard. Not only a crack shot but the new preacher-man of his people. Didn't that beat all?

Sister Edna Sunset's lovely face glowed proudly despite the deep sadness still clinging to her eyes. She never seemed more saintly.

She knew in her heart and soul that Martinius Rheinbeck

could rest in peace—now. His work had been done. He had passed on the torch. And David Bard—her David—had accepted it. Without complaint.

The Prodigal Son had indeed come home again.

There were barely thirty people left when the count was made at sundown. More than fifty Christian-born souls had perished as a result of the terrible fire and the attack of the renegade Indians. The loss of men, women, and children was beautified in words and prayers. Yet life still held meaning. For David Bard, a new resolve stiffened him—he had literally aged far beyond his nineteen years in a mere forty-eight hours. The spirit and ghost of Martinius Rheinbeck, as if speaking to him from the grave, was never very far away now.

That grave, true to David's word, was on the grassy hillock from which he and Link Hullar had performed their courageous rescue. And to mark the spot, Andy Beigel called on Frank Hamilton, an artist from Gloucester, Massachusetts, to fashion the words and a religious design on a slab of stone which would serve to designate this grave from all the others on hand. Hamilton, a bespectacled, kindly faced man, once Sister Edna Sunset had provided him with the necessary information and inscription desired, did a fine all-around job, indeed. The headstone read, in firm Gothic letters:

HERE LIES
MARTINIUS RHEINBECK
A MAN OF GOD
BORN 1809 DIED 1859
He Walked With the Good Lord.

Above and below the lettering, Frank Hamilton had chiseled out angel wings interlocking. It was lovely to behold. A work of art.

For all the others who had fallen, another huge common grave. Nothing seemed to matter anymore, for there was not a man now who was not a widower, hardly a woman who was not a widow, not a child—there were but a few left—who was not fatherless or motherless. It was a dark world indeed, that twentieth day of October, eighteen hundred and fifty-nine. David Bard conducted all the burial services from Martinius Rheinbeck's Bible, a book which now had become as necessary to him as the Navy Colt strapped to his side. He briefly wished that poet fellow Whitman had been there then to help form some pretty words to say over Martinius. But he did the best he could; he spoke from the heart; he read the Twenty Third Psalm once more, for he remembered how Martinius Rheinbeck had loved it. And Sister Edna Sunset, never leaving his side, sang "Rock of Ages" and "Nearer My God to Thee" more soulfully and beautifully than he had ever heard them before.

Link Hullar had scattered the vultures circling lazily overhead with a few well-aimed blasts from the shotgun.

Then finally, just after sunset, with everyone settling in for another night out in the open, with very little shelter, David asked Link to help him distribute the Bibles from the large crate in the Conestoga. Men had been sent to recover the game they had left behind in their race to save the town. Supper had been bountiful and there was a general uplifting of spirits. But the dead were still dead, and sorrow still acute, so David Bard knew the time had come for some restoration and hope from the words of the

Holy Bible. Richard Clear, Rusty Hevelin, and Andy Beigel could not have agreed more. David began to recognize the names and the faces of some of the others who had survived the twin disasters. Don Higgins, Al Tonik, Joe Lewandowski, Wooda Carr, Bob Sampson—all affable men. Good-hearted men, anxious to rebuild again, for their families and their futures. What was left of them—so many of their friends and neighbors had been slaughtered. Walter Miller, Amy Highland, Will Murray, Barbara Douglas, Lou Carlucci, the Fisher brothers—the list was endless. Like a roll call of the dead. One family alone, the McQueens, Dorothy McQueen and her three unmarried daughters, had all been wiped out that first day of the fire.

Yes, there was a lot to remember and a lot to forget.

If everybody was going to live again, rebuild again.

But the Good Lord willing, if everybody pitched in and helped, did what they could do, a town could rise again from this chaos. *Would* rise. Sister Edna Sunset was certain of that. With every ounce of her faith and being. He would not be able to make it without her. There was no doubt in David Bard's mind about that.

He knew now that he needed her in every way that a man can need a woman. His own woman.

"Edna, if I do this thing—*we* do this thing—carry on for Martinius—I'm going to need all the help you can give me."

"You know you have that without asking, David. I owe it to Martinius that his work and his words do not die."

"That's all well and good. But I'm also talking now about you and me. I want you with me. And not just in the daytime in front of all the folks."

She turned her back to him, unable to speak.

They were alone, standing alongside the wagon tongue of the Conestoga while the unharnessed horses grazed nearby on the grassy hillock close to Martinius Rheinbeck's final resting place.

"Edna? You hear what I said?"

"I heard you. But I will not come to you in the wagon. Not before all of them. In the eyes of God, it would not be right."

"I'm not asking you that, Sister Edna Sunset," he declared in a sterner voice than he intended. She turned then, her blue eyes searching his ardent face. "What are you asking me then, David?"

His smile was almost bleak now.

"I know I'm the new minister here. The preacher. Martinius said he could marry folks. Well, I can too. But I can't marry us. But seeing as how Richard Clear is—was— the mayor of Horsefall, he could marry us if I was to ask him."

"Were to ask him, David—were." Her eyes were shining. Radiant.

"All right—were. But I'm not going to ask him until you tell me how what I said sets with you. I know we only been acquainted for no more'n five days, but I feel like I've known you forever. You know?"

"I know," she breathed with a funny catch in her voice he had never heard before. "David . . ."

"I'm listening. And waiting for your word."

The cornflower-blue eyes yet shone, but there was a sadness in her voice now that said far more than he desired to hear.

"I will marry you, David Bard. I have never given myself to any man and I know now that you will be the one for me. But, dear David, please don't ask me to do this thing now. Not right away. Please ask me again—later. When you know this is the life you want, that I am the woman you truly want.''

"Edna, for God's sake—"

"Don't take the Lord's name in vain, and please hear me out. Do you think I could lie with you on the very night that Martinius Rheinbeck died? Think of that, David, and think of what it would say about me. And you—to all these good people we are now a part of. Oh, David—'' Her fingers went to his arm, pressed warmly. "You can never know how I long for you—ache for you—truly, never have I felt like this, but may I be everlastingly damned if I let that kind of love be spoiled by both of us acting like two greedy persons who couldn't wait for a more proper time and place.''

The unarguable words sank in, penetrated the soft layers of his brain, and suddenly, incredibly, he had thrown back his head and laughed. A hearty, young laugh, and before she could misinterpret his reaction, he took her two hands in his own, turned the palms upward and kissed them. "Ma would have loved you, Sister Edna Sunset. Pa, too. Same as I do right now with every bone in my body.''

Her gaze faltered; the blue eyes were puzzled.

"Then you understand—you'll do what I ask?"

He nodded, eyes twinkling. She was so lovely, so *right*.

" 'Course I will. You said you wanted me and that's all I really wanted to hear. And you're dead correct, Edna. We have to wait. For Martinius' sake, and our own. I'm sorry I didn't see that for myself. But I guess I'm still learning things.''

Sister Edna Sunset tilted her golden-haired head and

kissed him. Full on the mouth. He folded his arms around her and held her for a long, long time. For the first time in a great while, the world seemed like a beautiful place. Free of lynchings, murderous robbers, terrible fires, and renegade savages. And John Brown raids on arsenals.

"Thanks for loving me, Edna Sunset."

"Thank *you*, David Bard."

Neither of them could have known, as sweet as the air was now, that things were going to get a lot worse. Much worse.

All they did know was that they loved each other.

And that Martinius Rheinbeck must be smiling in his quiet grave.

Such is the eternal optimism of the very young.

God bless them both.

AM I MY BROTHER'S KEEPER?

There was no keeping track of the next few days, or all the rest of that week. A town had died and those who were left of its population had begun reconstruction with next to nothing to begin with—in fact, having to start all over again from figurative and literal scratch. But the spirit was there, the will, and the dedication, and with those three sterling virtues something was done. Things got accomplished, however difficult they were at the outset. Everybody rolled up their sleeves and dug in. Nobody held back. And soon enough signs of life and animation stirred on the scorched earth that had once been Horsefall.

No building was done, no erecting of shacks or shelter. That would have to come last. The first priority was food and protection from further attacks by whatever enemies there might be. Toward this end, Richard Clear showed the mettle and vigor which had obviously led to his selection as mayor in the first place. He quietly and firmly showed his hand for organization.

He assigned Link Hullar the daily chores of hunting for game and also fishing in any of the outlying streams and creeks. Several of the men accompanied Hullar, and the shotguns of Martinius Rheinbeck saw more service. Fortunately, there was a goodly supply of shells in the Conestoga. Hullar proved a veritable Daniel Boone and Nimrod combined. He never came back empty-handed, and the survivors of Horsefall began to have a daily ration of fresh meat and fresh fish. Water was also Link Hullar's business, and all kegs and barrels in camp began to be filled with regularity. The forest teemed with brooks and creeks whose water could be secured and boiled for sanitation.

Clear detailed Andy Beigel for the security of the camp. Beigel posted men all around the perimeter of the scorched area, two on each ridge in two-hour shifts so that an around-the-clock safety belt constantly ringed the area. He also made a count of guns and ammunition still left and announced an inventory of seven revolvers, one muzzle-loader, four rifles, and an assortment of hand knives. David Bard's shotguns and Navy Colt and horse pistol were not included in this total. Nor was the Bowie knife. There was roughly about one hundred rounds of ammunition left for all the handguns and something would have to be done about that.

Rusty Hevelin was sent into the forest with Wooda Carr, Bob Sampson, Joe Lewandowski, Don Higgins, and Al Tonik to see if any of the horses, cows, pigs and fowl which had taken off in terror during the fire could be recovered. Everyone had been too dazed that first day to think of doing just that. But now it seemed to make all the

sense in the world. "Land o' Goshen," Al Tonik exclaimed in wonder, "why didn't we think of this day
before yesterday when there was a better chance of finding
them?" Nobody answered him. And at this day's end, sure
enough, Hevelin's party came back to camp with one cow
in tow, three horses, four pigs, and a brace of chickens. All
the rest had either kept on running or been brought down by
other predators of the woods. It didn't matter. A rousing
cheer went up as Rusty, with his reddish Santa Claus
beard, came riding back on one of the horses, leading his
victorious hunters into camp.

As for the women, that was Sister Edna Sunset's department. As young as she was, the aura of quiet power that
surrounded her as well as her spiritual connection with the
Lord, sufficed to make every female around her yield to
her authority. She got the women busy mending torn
garments, helping her bake bread from the grain remaining
in the bags in the wagon. The females tended to the
children—there were but nine of them left—and as they
did, they began to clear away the rubble and debris of the
camp as best they could. In a short time a semblance of
order was restored to the scorched section of earth which
once had been a town. Sister Edna's sewing box with its
great supply of thread and needles came in mighty handy.
Some of the ladies hummed as they worked, in spite of the
aura of tragedy all around them—the huge community
graveyard and the individual mounds where the elderly
who had died now lay. Martinius Rheinbeck's stone glittered in the sunlight, reminding everyone of what had
happened here only a short while ago.

And soon enough horsemen rode in from the surrounding towns, bringing blankets, provisions, and extra arma-

ment. Word had traveled somehow, as it will in the
wilderness, and almost everyone within a radius of fifty
miles had now heard the story of the great fire, the raid of
the Fox braves, and the coming of a preacher-man and a
woman and a young lad who had a way with guns. The
horsemen were from Whitney—and then wagons rolled in
from Hazard and Blackey. And it seemed that everyone
and his brother wanted to help. Living and dying in the
wilderness was a common bond for all people who searched
for new land on which to build new homes.

David Bard could only marvel at all this, sensing once
again what Martinius Rheinbeck had meant about the in-
herent goodness in people and the unquenchable spirit of
Christian mankind. He began to feel even more strongly
about the Lord in his own mind. And as was his daily
custom now, he read the Bible each and every free moment he had. He was surrendering to its magic, its powerful words and lessons—and heeding Edna Sunset's advice,
though he longed for her mightily, now more than ever, he
made a visible show of sleeping on the ground outside the
Conestoga wagon while she was the mistress of its interior. Sure enough, he soon saw that all of his new neighbors and townspeople thought the better of him for the
gesture. Edna had never seemed more beautiful and desir-
able to him because of his staunch self-control.

Fortunately, the weather remained good: blue skies,
white clouds and cool winds, as if the Lord himself was
smiling down on all their efforts. Indian summer had never
been so pleasant.

And then, with everything in full swing and a sense of
worth and accomplishment filling every heart and soul,

trouble showed its ugly face. And it came from the most unexpected source.

A horseman rode into the area—an Indian fighter by the look of him, riding a dusty sorrel, sitting straight and firmly in the saddle, dressed in the same sort of buckskins that David Bard wore. He dismounted and made a beeline for the Conestoga wagon. Word traveled fast, and soon enough the strange horseman was surrounded by the men who counted in ravaged Horsefall. David Bard, Richard Clear, Rusty Hevelin, and Andy Beigel.

The newcomer measured his listeners before he uttered a single word, and they in turn inspected him from hat to boot. Each man liked what he saw. There was something about the stranger that augured command and great inner strength and, perhaps, pure courage.

He was of medium height, but broad shoulders tapered down to a trim, lithe figure that an Indian might have envied. The face was bronzed and somehow youthful despite the full, curling grey moustache and matching gray-streaked hair that hung to his shoulders, full-length. The eyes were a deep brown and unblinking. A straight nose and a sculpted chin showed a countenance to the world of men that clearly indicated a man who would not back down in a gunfight or run at the first sign of trouble. The easy, unhurried demeanor of the man betokened a life of living outdoors and surviving off the land. David Bard liked the look of him, as he saw the others did too. Still, there was something troubling about this stranger's sudden materialization from out of the blue.

Any man wearing a pair of revolvers with ivory handles with the butts reversed, indicating a specialist in the draw known as the "frontiersman's twist," commanded attention. Spanish boots, black leather with white patches, finished off his eye-catching figure. The stranger, realizing that protocol directed that he speak first, now did so in the laconic, quiet voice they all would have expected. Never had a voice so suited a man's appearance.

"You folks fixin' to put down roots here again?"

David nodded, almost smiling. "That's our aim, stranger. If you're asking to settle in with us, you're more than welcome."

"Can't do that. You can't, either." The words were bluntly spoken.

Richard Clear stirred, a touch of anger edging his words.

"What do you mean—and who are you, anyway? Federal marshal—"

"Didn't tell you at that, did I?" The newcomer's smile was thin. "They call me Hernon. Ed Hernon. Fast Ed, for a fact. Heard about you folks. The trouble you had. Well, now you got more."

Rusty Hevelin and Andy Beigel matched snorts of derision. "After what we been through?" Rusty shook his head. "Hernon, I hope you mean well telling us that. If you don't—"

Ed Hernon took no offense.

"Better explain myself." He took a beat and then continued in his calm way. "Those Injuns you run off—they're comin' back. This time they'll be maybe a hundred of them. You see those red devils who jumped you were renegades. From the Fox tribe. They know the shape you're in. What was left of them hooked up with another band of young bucks who quit their own tribes. There's lot of those in these parts. They're maybe two days' ride from you now, but they'll be here. You can stake your hair on that, friends.''

David frowned. ''We'll be ready for them then.''

Ed Hernon looked at him, almost pityingly.

''With but two dozen people and not enough guns? No way in hell, Preacher-Man. And you can't count on the folks from other towns to throw in with you. They got to look after their own people. No—the way I see it, your best bet is to move on out. Leave all this bad ground. That fire left things in no shape to rebuild. Believe me, I seen this happen before. You'll all be massacred. Them bucks got their paws on a lot of Army rifles. They'll be packin' more than bows and arrows and tomahawks this time.''

David Bard asked him then the only question worth asking.

''You know me then. And how do you know all this you're telling us, Mr. Hernon?''

''You're kinda damn famous now, son. Yes, I heard of you. Folks talked about the preacher who came to these parts with a beautiful female and a young man in buck-skins.'' The dark brown eyes were somehow approving. ''I also heard how old Rheinbeck died and how you saved the town with some fancy shooting. Also, I liked what I heard. That's why I'm here. I want to see you folks outa this mess.''

''But we want to rebuild here,'' Richard Clear protested. ''Horsefall's gone, of course, but we'll raise a new town. Give it a new name. We can't let Indians run us off now.''

Ed Hernon lost his smile.

''You'll have to. If you're thinkin' of help from the U.S. Army, you can forget that, too. The nearest post is five days' ride from here. Nothing's gonna stop those red bucks from hittin' you again—and hittin' you for keeps.''

Andy Beigel's dour face changed into a suspicious scowl. ''Something's on your mind, Hernon. Why are you telling us all this? What's your stake?''

''Tell you what, friend. Pull out. You've got maybe thirty folks to pack. You got yourself maybe six wagins now, thanks to your neighbors—and some horses. Enough food and supplies. Move out while the moving's good. Forget about this burned-out, dead ground. Build somewhere else. There's a big country out there. Bustin' to be filled. I'm asking for the job of wagon master. And scout. I got the experience and the credentials. Also, I'm hankering to move on. The Colorado Territory, maybe. I don't suggest Kansas. Too all-fired bloody and mixed-up now, what with this slavery business. That's why I'm here. To do you a good turn and same time find me a good reason for pushing further west. That good enough for you?''

David Bard, Richard Clear, Rusty Hevelin, and Andy Beigel all exchanged glances. But it was left to David Bard to answer him.

''How do you know about the Indians coming back again?''

''That's my business. Told you I'm a scout. Did a lot of time with the Army on the frontier. Gave it up. Rules and regulations ain't for me.''

''Why do you call yourself Fast Ed?''

''Everybody else calls me that.'' The gun butts never seemed more prominent. Ed Hernon smiled. Bleakly again. ''Hope you never have to find out why, Preacher. I've killed a lot of men.''

No one doubted him on that. He stated his credentials

with quiet authority. No bravado whatsoever. David Bard pondered, then shook himself and looked at the others. "Well. You heard him. Same as me. What do you think we oughta do?"

Clear's normally benign face was troubled now. "I can't say right off. This bears a powerful lot of thinking over. It's too big a decision to make in five minutes. Rusty, what's your notion?"

" 'Fraid I feel as you do," Rusty Hevelin sighed. "Sure had my mind set on settling in here again and building her back up to a nice little town. Even was thinking up new names for the place. Like calling her *Rheinbeck* maybe, in honor of the preacher we lost."

"Yes," David agreed. "That would have been fittin' and proper. Andy—what's your reckoning?"

The retired railroad man shrugged, his eyes thoughtful.

"Man comes to you to warn you about something, stands to reason you oughta listen to him. I don't wanta leave, but if we have to, we have to, I guess. No sense in bucking facts."

"Hernon," David Bard saw his duty once more. "Mind if we talk about this in private for a while?"

"Take your time," Fast Ed Hernon agreed, moving away, his hands swinging freely, not far from the ivory handles of his pistols. "I'll set over by that rock and rest a spell. Been in the saddle since Glade Spring."

"Thank you. And whatever we decide, we're much obliged for your advice. And Hernon?"

"Yeah?" The way he turned easily, shoulder shifting, legs straddled, they knew more than ever ever that he was a man who had faced other men down on dusty streets, along the trail, and in saloons. There was gunfighter in him, too. An air of menace.

"Have you any word of John Brown and the raid at Harpers Ferry? Happened some ten days ago."

Fast Ed Hernon's eyes lidded, as if he found the question a strange one from a young man who had only recently taken over the Lord's work from his dead teacher. None of the others thought the query odd. They all assumed David was testing Hernon somehow.

"Yeah, heard about that. Old Brown kinda shot up the arsenal, but they stopped him. He's in irons now. Him and his people. Only they won't stay in irons too long."

"What do you mean?" David asked, his brain leaping.

"They're fixin' to hand the old hell-raiser," Fast Ed Hernon drawled slowly. "Come December."

With that, he turned again and sauntered toward the slope of the rising ground, to the self-same projection of stone where David and Edna Sunset had suddenly discovered how they felt about each other. But David was not thinking about that now. He was thinking of destiny and fate and the God who had delivered him to Martinius Rheinbeck and the only woman he knew he would ever love. Instead of a gallows platform and a hangman's noose. Like that poor black boy. The ways of Providence were very strange indeed.

Yet there was no more time to dwell on John Brown.

He and Richard Clear and Rusty Hevelin and Andy Beigel surely had to make a decision of staying put or pulling out. Some thirty lives were in the balance, however they decided.

"Well," David Bard said crisply, once Fast Ed Hernon had reached his rock, "let's get this matter decided."

Andy Beigel took the floor, in his dour way.

"It's bound to come to a vote between all of us. So each of us better get his say in. All right, I'll start first with the way I see it. 'Course, we're gonna have to ask all the others how they feel, but it stands to reason we got to decide for ourselves first. That way we'll present one decision at least."

No one disagreed with him. They all waited. Beigel grunted.

"Now, here's the way this situation seems to me. . . ."

They all listened with rapt attention.

The conference that ensued, the arguments, the judgments, the alternatives, the conditions, took a full hour. When they had done, they had at last found their common answer.

It was not an easy answer to come by.

Saying good-bye to something, taking leave of a way of life for a new, unknown one, is never easy.

But the verdict of the committee of four was unanimous.

When David Bard sought out Ed Hernon at the rock, Richard Clear, Rusty Hevelin, and Andy Beigel had returned to their own billets. He was taken back a little to see the buckskinned frontiersman in what seemed like a close conclave with Sister Edna Sunset. A quick stab of something strange flared in his mind. Edna and Fast Ed Hernon looked so good together, even though he had to be years older. Say, in his late thirties. David recognized his own symptoms. Jealousy, of all things. It was childish of him, he knew, but the ways of love were still far too new to him. So he kept his face poker-blank and joined the two of them, smiling only with his eyes. Fast Ed Hernon was leaning indolently against the rock, a corncob pipe clamped between his white teeth, puffing contentedly, arms folded. Sister Edna Sunset was standing before him, head bent, talking in a low voice. They turned as he approached, and Edna flashed him a gorgeous smile.

"Powwow over, Preacher-Man?" The query was typically curt.

"Call me David Bard, Hernon," David said without inflection. "I see you've both gotten acquainted."

Edna Sunset nodded, tugging a loose strand of hair away from her brow. "Mr. Hernon was explaining to me what's been going on."

"That is keerect, Bard," Fast Ed Hernon said mildly enough. "And I hope for all your hides, you made the right decision."

"Like all things," David Bard replied with a rationality that Martinius Rheinbeck would have admired and applauded, "the right or wrong of it we won't know until later on. Leastways, we all threw in with your notion, Hernon. Now all we gotta do is ask the folks if they'll go along with our thinking."

Edna Sunset seemed glad at the news.

"Thank the Lord. It's always best to move on from a place where there has been so much trouble and unhappiness. I'm sure it will be for the best and I'm almost certain all the others will feel the same way. It will be hard for them, leaving their dead, but they can always come back."

David Bard had figured she would be all for going. But now it upset him a trifle that she had given in so readily. Perhaps it was because it was the idea of the moustached, long-haired, dark-eyed scout standing alongside her now, tamping the tobacco down in the corncob pipe. "The sooner you ask them, the better, Bard," Fast Ed Hernon suggested. "That way I can see to settin' up a wagon train worth takin' into the new territory. That's never an easy job. I wanta outfit this bunch for a long, hard haul."

"It will be done," David said flatly. "And remember this, if we go and there is a wagon train, I'm the one in charge. It can't be any other way, Hernon. I want that understood here and now."

"Wouldn't have it any other way, David Bard." Fast Ed Hernon tipped his hat in Sister Edna's direction and put his pipe back into his mouth. "I'll see to my horse. And I'll see you both later. California, here I come." With that, he was gone again, sauntering off in his casual, unhurried way. Sister Edna stared after him. David studied her, trying to read her face.

"David—how does Mr. Hernon strike you?"

"He's been through a lot more than me, Edna. Must be a good man with a gun, a horse, and just about everything else. Leastways, he came to us to help us. So we're gonna make good use of him."

"I'm glad, then." Her eyes warmed him. "You've taken on a lot, you have. Martinius would be proud of you. I'm proud. You've made a grand impression on these people. I've heard them—they can't believe you're such a young man."

He smiled sheepishly. "Getting older by the day, Edna. Trouble has a way of aging a fellow. But I'm glad, too. We'll be together, and that sets a lot with me. Going west with you, Edna Sunset, may just be all that I'll ever want out of this life."

She stared back at him, without turning away or blushing. When she answered him, her voice was low, even and as right as the rain on a dry country. "*Whither thou goest, I will go . . .thy people shall be my people*—do you know that, David?"

"I do. Ruth and Naomi in the Good Book. That's what Naomi said—and—you see, I been reading the Bible every chance I have." He shook his head. "A couple of weeks ago I wouldn't know that. But Martinius Rheinbeck changed me about a lot of things."

"God rest him," she breathed fervently. "He was a great man."

"Yes," David Bard said. "He was. For a fact."

There was no more to be said.

Now they had to start thinking about moving out. Bag and baggage, the whole kit and kaboodle. That would not be easy at all.

But first the people had to be asked. Every one of them. They had to vote, too.

Fast Ed Hernon was right. It was move out or stay and die. David Bard had little doubt how that vote would go. The way west was the route to salvation.

Maybe it was the Lord's way, also.

THE WAY WESTWARD

Whatever he truly was or had been or would prove to be in the end, Fast Ed Hernon was a wagon master supreme. Once the survivors of Horsefall decided in the affirmative to go along with their new preacher-man, there was no stopping the quiet-faced scout with the guns worn reverse-fashion. As an organizer and outfitter, preparing some thirty people for a long drive through the wilderness of space, forests, mountains, and streams and rivers, he knew what he was doing. David Bard accepted his expertise and experience without question, as everyone else did. Andy Beigel, watching the buckskinned scout in action, moving men and supplies about, rigging the wagons and assigning tasks and permanent jobs to the personnel, remarked dourly: "That jasper's done this before. You can tell. Never make a wrong move, does he? Wonder if he ever worked for the railroad?"

Rusty Hevelin guffawed. "No railroad ever held that man. He's a loner. You can tell by his manner. But I'll say this—I'm right glad to have him. Knows what he's doin' and that's a heap."

Richard Clear agreed. "So long as David wants him. That's good enough for me."

It was good enough for everybody else, too, and miraculously, in a mere ten hours following the general decision to leave the scorched earth of Horsefall, a wagon train was ready. There were six wagons, not all Conestogas, but wagons just the same outfitted for the trail, with plentiful barrels of water and a reasonable supply of provisions of all kinds.

There weren't enough horses, of course, for personal use, but somehow Ed Hernon corraled one rider for each wagon. An outrider who could serve as scout and protection, too. No vote was necessary about this. Hernon selected Richard Clear, Rusty Hevelin, Andy Beigel, and Link Hullar for these, with David Bard on a strawberry roan and Ed Hernon on his familiar sorrel. Link Hullar volunteered to ride rear-guard behind the wagons. The frontiersman approved of this when David told him what a fine shot Link was.

Each of the wagons was overcrowded, but that had to be. Sister Edna Sunset took three of the orphaned children, two boys and a girl, to make the journey in the big Conestoga. David did not demur. It would help him keep his distance from Sister Edna. There was enough to think about with the long haul and the threat of those redskins still with them. As for the route the wagon train would follow, Fast Ed Hernon laid it out for all of them, in one last council, before the long journey began. He didn't use a map or refer to any chart of any kind. His dark-eyed smile was almost fatherly.

"We're moving out due west. Take my word for it, I know every foot of the way, like the back of my hand. There's an old wagon trail that cuts across right through the Cumberlands to Missouri. And then it's Kansas and then the Colorado Territory. There's a way to go around Kansas—told you, that's a hot spot right now—but we can cross that bridge when we come to it. First thing we got to do is clear out of here. Those fellows with feathers on their heads are gettin' closer every hour we stay here."

"Won't they follow us, Hernon?" David asked, "when they get here and find us gone?"

"Maybe so, maybe not. Can't always tell what an Indian will think. But we'll be better off moving away from them, no matter how you look at it. Fact is, they won't know what we did or where we are. I know how not to leave too many tracks."

"All right, then. We're ready when you are."

"That's it, then. Tell your people to mount up and be ready to move out when I give the word."

David Bard complied thankful that the Lord had sent them a Fast Ed Hernon, whatever he was. And as activity and excitement traveled along the line of six wagons, he spurred the roan over to the sloping hillside for one last look at Martinius Rheinbeck's grave. The slab of upright stone with its beautifully etched epitaph seemed to look up at him. He swept off his buckskin hat, closed his eyes, and murmured a silent prayer. Then he opened them, and through a moist veil of sudden sadness, he said aloud to himself. And to Martinius Rheinbeck. "God bless you forever, Martinius Rheinbeck. I'll never forget you. I'd never be able to—hope we meet again someday."

With that, he turned the roan and galloping back took up his position beside the lead wagon. Sister Edna Sunset stared at him, her strong hands firmly intertwined with the ribbons of the reins. Behind her, the three children, the boys and the girl, no older than ten, gazed in awe at him, their eyes round and shining.

"I said good-bye to him while you were with the council, David."

"Figured you did. It wasn't easy."

"I know."

"We'll come back someday. I promise. And put flowers on that grave. And maybe build a church here—he'd like that."

Sister Edna Sunset smiled proudly.

"You'll do it, David. If you say you will."

Five minutes later Fast Ed Hernon, face grim, twisted in his saddle, raised his right arm and bellowed in a loud, clear voice that carried down the line of waiting wagons. "MOVE OUT! KEEP THOSE WAGONS NO FURTHER THAN TWENTY FEET APART. FORWARD, HO-O-O-O!" Never had the old cavalry command to move been uttered with such authority and urgency. It was a cry to remember, rising over the forest of canvas-covered wagons, topping the wind, reaching to the gray skies overhead. October was in its final days and autumnal colors and shades of brown and red were touching all the leaves.

The six wagons moved forward, each of their occupants aflame with expectation and hope and curiosity. The way westward was ever an adventure, always a perilous undertaking, continually frightening with its newness and possibilities.

For David Bard, it seemed the beginning of another life.

He was truly Martinius Rheinbeck now.

A leader of a flock, taking them to a new land.

With only the Bible to guide him, and the woman he wanted with all his heart and soul. It was getting harder and harder to look at her every day and keep his thoughts clear and his hands still. His heart always beat faster around her. But now the single most important thing was to strike this camp and move out and find some kind of Promised Land for his people. These homeless wanderers.

David Bard knew he wasn't Moses.

But he sure felt like him that October day.

And before journey's end he was to feel like someone far worse. Like another David, that famous king who wrote the "Song of Solomon" in the Bible, but also a man who sent a soldier into battle, one of his generals, hoping he would be killed, because he also loved King David's wife Bathsheba.

The Bible was right.

As it always was.

The soldier this time was Fast Ed Hernon.

The wagon train made camp some thirty miles from its point of departure. The wagon master picked a location which could not have been bettered. By a running stream, close to the shelter of a low-lying ridge of mountains. The camp was completely encircled with trees, not too far off the trail. The long, hard journey had been without event, spiced only with a light rain which had not been bothersome at all. The flatlands had fallen away, yielding to draws, valleys, and softly rising earth. Ed Hernon had led all the way, hardly talking to anyone, maintaining his lead in the vanguard, riding back once for a cup of hot coffee and then returning to his post. A shot rang out once, and everybody jumped fearfully, but it was only Link Hullar in the rear chasing off a wolf pack that had inquisitively come too close. Kentucky faded into the distance. Missouri opened up, spreading a carpet of green in the twilight.

The evening meal went off without a hitch, the women led by Edna Sunset whipping up a fine, wholesome dinner of beans, corn cakes, and bacon. The children romped and played, as if there never had been a Horsefall. It was nice to see, and hear. David Bard performed the grace for the good supper, as Martinius Rheinbeck had done. No one seemed to mind; in fact, all the smiling faces seemed to welcome the custom. For where God was, even in this wilderness, there was hope and comfort. The young 'un knew his Bible, too, by the sound of him. Horsefall's survivors began to breathe easy again.

After supper there was no revelry or socializing of any kind. It was Ed Hernon's considered opinion that everybody would have to hold off on such goings-on until they were all pretty damn sure they had lost their Indian pursuers. Nobody minded. Everyone was tired from the long day on the trail. The campfire was doused and the sentries were posted and everybody turned in for the night. There was no moon, no stars. The sky was a dark curtain.

With the camp asleep, David Bard slipped quietly to the running stream and behind a copse of foliage, divested himself of the buckskins and boots, and eased himself into the very cold water. He stroked quietly, letting the clear liquid enter every pore. It was a tonic, cleansing, purifying, after so many days of dust and dirt and grime. Too, the water cooled his hot body, the one that ached and yearned for a woman—the woman he wanted.

Yes, there was God, there was love, and there was purity.

But there was also youth and impatience and natural selection. And just this one time, youth would be served. It had to be.

David Bard lay on his back in the stream, staring up at the dark sky, not moving, thinking slowly, carefully. Not a sound came from the direction of the camp no more than a hundred feet away. And then came the shock of his lifetime. Only his shock was the penultimate in niceness, in goodness. In pleasure.

A slender, shapely shadow loomed above him. Close. Long hair trailed down, touching him. Warm hands touched his shoulders. He jumped, reflexively, but the warm hands pressed him down. And a face he could not see but one he knew better than his own, lowered to him. And a soft, urgent voice whispered, "I am here, David—I have taken off all my clothes."

Warm lips kissed him almost savagely. The coolness, the coldness of the water, vanished. Her body with its ample bosom and full, curved womanly contours melded to him with sudden strength and force. "I can wait no longer—I am weak."

"Edna," he breathed, wonderingly, hardly able to speak—his arms already molding her to his own outline, every inch and ounce of him now riotously aflame.

"Ohh, don't speak—do, David, do. We will talk about this later. I love you, David Bard. With all my heart and soul!"

He needed to hear no more. Exultantly he rose, sweeping her drippingly aloft in his strong arms. He burrowed his face into her damp bosom and stalked for shore. There was a bower of trees there, a small, bosky place where one could lie, unseen by the camp. He set her down. She lay beneath him. Full-length, arms outstretched. In the gloom, the cornflower-blue eyes, the golden-blonde hair, the lovely mouth—touched with darkness, they were somehow more glorious than ever. "Edna, my God . . ." he whispered thickly, certain his heart would burst, his head explode.

"Dear David . . ." she said softly, her voice coming up to him in a heavenly haze of darkness. "Please, David— before I lose my courage."

He fell on her then, beyond all recalling.

The moment had come. The time was here—his and Sister Edna's hour for loving.

They came together hungrily, yearningly, lustily.

It would never ever be this right again, this natural, this preordained. If there were angels in heaven, they had to be smiling. All was right with the world—God was in his heaven, too.

And it was all happening under a Missouri sky.

In a land where neither of them had ever been before in their lives. A new country, a different world.

Somehow, that too was altogether fitting and proper.

Long afterward—neither of them could have said how long—they lay locked together under the heavy blanket Sister Edna Sunset had brought with her. There was utter silence on all sides. It would have been difficult to believe a wagon train stood at rest so close by. And yet it was indeed as if they were both alone in the world. The first time must be always like this, David Bard thought. For everyone who had ever been in love. The night had grown cooler, but neither of them noticed that, either. There was a universe of warmth and wonder in the simple act of lying together like this.

The heaving, the pumping, the crushing had stopped. The great passionate tide that had swept them both along in its current had slowed, ebbed, and peacefully subsided. But the wonder remained.

Their faces were close, their lips a breath apart.

And the aroma of fresh flowers and honey was in his nostrils forever. She had her special fragrance and he knew it for all time now. It was something he never would forget, no matter what happened. Come Hades, perdition, and Indians and plague and famine.

"David," she murmured, "was it the same for you—what we did?"

"It was the way it was meant to be," he answered deeply. "As I knew it was going to be." It was funny, almost, how carefully he was pronouncing his words. "I'm never going to forget this night."

Her sigh wafted over him, fanning his naked shoulder.

"I was all filled up with you—I felt like I was going to burst—and then—then—oh, God, David—it's so good."

"I know."

"And it isn't as if we're not marrying. How I wish Martinius were here so I could tell him and he could tell me how right it all was. I know in my heart the Lord understands."

"He understands. Reading the Good Book convinces me of that. We're set for the same trail in this life, Edna. That makes anything we do together right. Anything that doesn't hurt anyone else. 'Sides, I love you and you love me. That's got to make it right in the eyes of the Lord. And anybody else.''

She snuggled closer, as if that were possible. Their bodies stirred again. She squirmed like an uneasy kitten. "Oh, David, I *am* shameless; I feel like a wanton—those women you read about in the Bible and hear tell of.''

"Then I'm glad you are." He fell silent, and she stopped moving too. Her cool fingers found his face, stroked the hair along his chin. "What are you thinking about, David?''

"Ma. Pa. They must have been like this—they loved each other a heap. I was thinking how he cried when she took sick and died—never forgot that. Never will.''

"I know," she said, remembering her own twin calamities.

They kissed each other. Quietly, tenderly. His heart was in full ascension, hers was just as high. They were both soaring on the wings of a deep, mutual love—the kind that is not yet selfish and motivated by anything else from the outside world.

A dry twig crackled suddenly in the darkness. In all that stillness and solitude it sounded as loud as any pistol shot to one who was awake. Edna Sunset gasped and David Bard reached quickly for the butt of the Navy Colt thrusting from the gun belt close by his hand. He cautioned her to silence, and waited, alert for the smallest noise or movement from the brush behind them.

And then came a running sound, footfalls racing away through the thicket. David relaxed, smiling. Some woods critter, a small one, had come across them and wisely headed in another direction. No human being could have made such a light sound. But the warning served. It was too late and too dark to remain where they were.

"Probably a rabbit, maybe a woodchuck or gopher, but
we'd best turn in." She nodded, agreeing, undecided, but
in the end she kissed him again. A long, ardent kiss. Then
they said no more to each other, dressed as quickly and
quietly as possible, and slipped back to the Conestoga
wagon—Edna Sunset to return to her charges within and
David to unfurl his bedroll on the earth below the wagon,
pulling down the rolled-up canvas buckled to either side of
the wagon which formed a lean-to, tentlike arrangement
that would keep him covered should it rain. He and Edna
Sunset both went to sleep with stars in their eyes and
delight in their hearts.

Neither of them had been aware of the silent, watching
figure in the buckskins that had taken up a position in the
upper branches of a dead cottonwood tree beyond the
perimeter of the camp. A figure that moved as silently as
any Indian could. A man who was no stranger to anything
in the wide open spaces of a growing country.

Fast Ed Hernon, his unlit corncob pipe clamped rigidly
between his white teeth, a rifle crooked in his right arm,
had seen the two young people returning to their wagon
from the direction of the running stream. Fast Ed Hernon
was not one to jump to conclusions. But he was also a
man, and he had seen Sister Edna Sunset and he had
quietly noted how David Bard looked at her. Like a moon-
calf bit with the bug. The love bug. And her—well, he had
seen bitches in heat, too. They both had all the signs, and
Fast Ed Hernon was a reader of signs if he was anything at
all. The way these two felt about one another could cause
some trouble along the way—that was for a fact. A man in
charge of a bunch of folks like young David Bard was had
no business feeling the way he did about just *one* of his

followers. Not when he was responsible for so many more. The time could come when he'd think of the lovely lady first and not the wagon train. Fast Ed Hernon was not going to let that happen. He knew now he was going to keep a weather eye fixed on both the young preacher-man and his lady love.

Not that he could blame the young buck.

The lady was the most beautiful woman he had ever eyed in all his born days. He had seen a painting in a saloon once, back in Pennsylvania; the kind they hung back of the bar to make the customers keep on drinking. A woman in feathers and little else—well, Edna Sunset put that painted lady to shame. And the painted lady had been a real beauty. An angel, almost. The painting had been called *Lady Margaret of Owens* and when he asked the bartender with the handlebar moustache about that, the answer he got was: "Some English tinhorn named Owens come in here and sold it to me. Said he was a painter once, over there in England. Said his wife posed for the picture. He was some kind of lord, he said, but I didn't care about that. The rags he was wearing, who'd believe him? Anyway, I liked the painting and I took it. Gave him twenty U.S. dollars for it. Never saw hide nor hair of him again— don't matter. All the customers love the painting and Lady Margaret. They toast her all the time."

Fast Ed Hernon had loved her, too. As an impossible dream, a woman never to be found in the flesh. In reality.

Until now.

In the quiet of the night he remained in the tree, keeping his watch, his eyes alert, his senses finely tuned. For danger.

He still wasn't too sure about those renegade red men he

yet expected to come. Over a hundred. A war party that size would be no laughing matter. He hoped the trail he had decided upon, an unknown one, a rougher one much later on, had fooled the damn scalp collectors. He had no love for Indians, in spite of their sometimes legitimate grievances. They had no call butchering whites the way they did and making souvenirs out of heads, hair, and bones. He had seen too many grisly remainders of Indian raids in his time as a scout, Army man, and saddle drifter. He had had a bellyful.

So he remained awake while everyone but the other sentries slept. He did not light the corncob pipe. It would have given off a telltale glow in the darkness.

He tried not to think about Lady Margaret of Owens. Or Sister Edna Sunset.

It was none too easy. None too easy at all.

Fast Ed Hernon, for all his self-determined loner life, was a very lonely man. No woman had ever been his. Not for more than a day, at any rate, in some godforsaken town, wherever he happened to hang his hat and take off his boots.

So he stayed put in his tree, rifle ready. A statue on guard. And tried not to think about what could have been. Or might be. That was the most difficult thing of all.

Benjamin Franklin had written that at night all cats were gray. So it was with all men in the small, lonely hours of any night. All men were brothers when they were lonely. White or red men.

Memories could ruin a fellow, as Fast Ed Hernon well knew.

The night wore on, stretching into the first gray streaks of dawn. Gray, ghostly light filtered over the low-lying mountain range and the tall, dense forest. The new day was coming up.

Ed Hernon had not closed his eyes once.

"Do you wish to make out a will, John Brown?"

"No, I do not."

"We will not ask you again, man. Think of your wife and the children remaining to her."

"Go away and leave me in peace. And to my God. Who should be your God, but you know him not."

"Very well. If that is how you feel, we won't ask you again, though six more weeks are left before you go to the gallows and your Maker."

"As it has been decreed, so shall it be. The sins of this unholy land will live behind me. I have done what I could. I do not fear your noose. Or your so-called justice. Go, now. Leave me!"

When they had gone, the priest with the white collar and the officious man with the muttonchop whiskers, John Brown sat down on his bare prison cot and placed his head in his hands. He struggled mightily not to give in to despair and faintheartedness. His craggy face had grown thinner since his capture, his beard yet whiter from the first day of his incarceration. His eyes were pale candles now, as if their inner fire had flamed low. He would die, he knew, and his only true fear was that the abomination known as slavery would continue. Go on until there would be no stopping to the calamity it was bound to bring forth. North against South, brother against brother. American against American.

Men would fight; boys, too—youths as young as David Bard had been. David Bard—for one long moment, John Brown was reminded of the lad they had lost on their sweeping run into the arsenal at Harpers Ferry. They never had learned what had happened to David Bard. David, who had been so eager, so filled with enthusiasm and bravery and rage for the good fight against slavery.

John Brown raised his head from his hands. His eyes glowed with the spirit of yesterday. Of old. Those eyes were not quite normal. They never would be.

Outside his stone-walled cell, he could hear the sound of a jew's harp playing. One of the other prisoners breaking the drudgery and weariness of imprisonment with music, with a Jew's harp, as it had come to be called. Aye, the Jews. They who began the workings of the Bible, the Old Testament, before they took the wrong path.

John Brown smiled, as despondent as he was.

The strains wafting down the corridor were all too familiar to him. A lament of the Negroes in the field, a song of slavery, a paean to another form of prisonhood—the melody known as "Old Black Joe," written by one Stephen Foster, a man who had fought slavery in his own inimitable way. A song of protest, all in all.

Gone are the days when my heart was young and gay;
Gone are my friends from the cotton fields away;
Gone from this earth to a better land I know;
I hear their gentle voices calling . . .
Old Black Joe. . . .
I'm coming, I'm coming, for my head is bending low . . .
I hear those gentle voices calling . . .

John Brown began to weep. Softly, quietly. Not for himself. He was beyond self-pity. But for America. And the world. And all the Old Black Joes everywhere, whose name was legion.

MISSOURI MADNESS

When the wagon train rolled on the next day, everyone had a good chance to see how Fast Ed Hernon had gained his soubriquet. There was no longer any reason to doubt the reverse pistols worn for the frontiersman's-twist draw. Hernon had halted the wagons before a box canyon and to no one's surprise ordained that the train would bypass the canyon, despite the excellent shelter it would afford for a camp. But Hernon was too wise in the ways of the trail and Indians to place the wagons in a spot which afforded only one exit—literally the same way the wagons went in. So he led his charges around the canyon and chose a site a few miles further on. Everyone was glad for the halt. It was time to noon again. And Missouri was proving endlessly more pleasurable than Kentucky for a trail drive. There were rivers, lakes, and streams aplenty, and the wilds were alive with game for Link Hullar's trusty rifle.

Better still, there had been no sign at all of their pursuers. Their luck was holding. Fast Ed Hernon was gaining admiration all around, and his reputation was to grow even greater soon enough. But David Bard and Edna Sunset, greeting the new day that morning, a clear, cooler day, were still caught up in the wondrous thing that had bound them together the night before. She looked at him almost shyly, and he in turn could only smile at her from his saddle. The children were gabbling excitedly, pointing out to each other each new hill and stream, every animal that came into view before rushing off brightened, into the forests. David murmured, "Good morning, Edna. Looks like a mighty fine day."

"Yes, doesn't it, David."

That was all that was said, but their tones spoke volumes, and Edna went happily back to her morning chores while David rode up and down the line, checking on things. Everybody seemed in a good mood and it augured well for a good day on the trail. Kentucky now, and Horsefall, was getting dimmer and dimmer in all minds. That was the way it was when men pushed on toward new horizons.

It was while everyone was sitting around, eating the midday meal of fried fish, beans, and coffee, that Diane Sampson emitted a fierce scream, and gathering up her skirts, she leaped back, pointing to the ground. A rattlesnake was slithering along the hard earth, heading away from the campfire toward the children. Everyone froze for a second, but not Fast Ed Hernon who chanced to be trotting by on the sorrel. Nobody saw the lightning draw, but everyone heard the booming blast of his pistol, and suddenly the snake's head was no longer attached to its length of ropelike body. Shaken, everyone cheered the feat, and Richard Clear marveled aloud to Rusty Hevelin. "I never even saw him pull that gun—on my oath!"

Hevelin's crafty, wise eyes glittered in awe, also.

"That rattler didn't either, Richard."

After that, no one questioned Fast Ed Hernon's credentials for leading a wagon train westward. But the scout accepted all congratulations with a curt nod and spurred his mount away to the lead wagon. There he joined David Bard and Edna Sunset and the unhitched horses grazing on grass. They had seen and heard all and they too added their compliments. Ed Hernon waved further words aside and leaned down from his saddle. His expression was rather grim. Though his eyes still held an odd gleam of something that had everything to do with what he knew of the midnight swim of Edna Sunset and David Bard. "Something we have to talk about, Brother Bard. And it won't wait."

"Listening, Hernon. You look mighty serious."

"Didn't want to scare the folks, unnecessarily. But we're getting deep into Indian country. Closer we get to the center of the state, we're bound to see some red faces."

"Hostiles?"

Ed Hernon's smile was very nearly amused. But not quite.

"Told you before. There's friendlies and there's hostiles. But they don't wear signs saying what they are. So best we avoid them when we can."

"I'm all for that. What are you asking me to do?"

"This is Osage country. And Shawnee. Maybe Wichita, and we could run into Comanches the further west we travel. Thing is, we got to be on double-guard now. I thought you ought to tell the ones who oughta know. Clear, Hevelin, Beigel. Figure it will set better coming from the leader of the flock.''

"All right. Anything you say." David read no sarcasm in the designation given him by the main scout. "Are there any other preparations we can make—we have enough firearms and men who can shoot."

"Nothing but to tell you this—if they attack us on the trail where there's open country, you pull your wagon around and everybody makes a circle. You understand? That way we shoot from all sides at them. Injuns like to ride around in circles. They got no sense about things like that. And it's the only defense that will give us a shooting chance." Hernon made a ring with his hands, indication how the wagons should be aligned. "We're too far off from any forts and settlements. That's why I picked this route. It was our best chance to get through this country without running into our red brothers. But there's always a chance we will.''

David Bard took Sister Edna's hand, for she had suddenly seemed frightened. The bright blue eyes were alarmed. David knew she was thinking of the children and not of herself. From his saddle, Fast Ed Hernon deemed her twice as lovely as Lady Margaret of Owens. If there ever had been such a woman, indeed.

"Hernon, how far you aiming to take us?"

"Clear across Missouri, like I said."

"I'll go along with you on that. But—remember. When we reach a place that's proper for a settlement, where these people can set down and dig in and I can build a church for them—that's the end of the line. Will you remember that?''

''That's the deal we made, Brother Bard, and I'll keep it so long as we keep our scalps on.''

''Just wanted to say it one more time, Hernon. So there's no mistake and no hard feelings later on.''

''You're the preacher, Brother Bard.''

When he rode off, tipping his wide-brimmed hat once more to Edna Sunset, David watched him with mild misgivings. Edna saw the look on his face and touched his arm gently.

''You don't trust him, do you, David?''

''You can tell that, huh?''

''It's right there on your face. And you talk different to him than you do the others—like you were trying to match him.''

David Bard laughed. ''No, I don't trust him completely. He's a loner and he came to us. You saw how good he is with that gun of his. And he wants to get someplace. And I got a feeling somehow he wants that place to be one of his own choosing. Not mine, not ours. But—I'm glad he's thrown in with us. We'll need a man like him if it comes to Indian trouble. And whatever else the Good Lord has planned for us.'' He turned to her and lost the smile. His eyes grew tender. ''Can you see what's in my face now, Edna?''

''Yes, David. And thank you.''

Again his blood raced at sight of her. His heart slammed more loudly. She saw that, too, in her divining way, and she moved off from him, her lovely face happy and content with the knowledge.

''I love you, David Bard,'' she almost whispered and

abruptly walked away from him. He did not stop her. Not
in broad daylight with the whole camp up and about,
bustling like a beehive.

A camp which had completed its noon meal and was
now loading up again to hit the trail once more. David
Bard also returned to the things he had to do. He was very
pleased to note that a lot of the travelers were spending
more and more time reading the little Bibles that he and
Link Hullar had distributed before this long journey had
begun. Even Link was thumbing his own copy more often
than usual. David saw all this as a good sign.

The Good Book might help them all through the
wilderness.

Spiritual strength was just as valuable as any rifle or
canteen of water or sack of flour. *Hear me, O Lord . . .*

Maybe more so if you were going to encounter Indians.

Frank Hamilton, the jovial artist who had done such a
fine job on Martinius Rheinbeck's tombstone, had been
making a lot of sketches and drawings as the journey
progressed. Edna Sunset had found them a joy to behold,
but Fast Ed Hernon had found a better way for Hamilton to
spend his time. He put the man to work doing trail maps,
marking the way they had come, signifying milestones and
landmarks and anything that would benefit future expedi-
tions along this heretofore uncharted passage across the
fair state of Missouri. It seemed a fine idea to David Bard,
too. Frank Hamilton was a demon with a drawing pencil in
his hand.

When the morning of the first of November dawned, Fast
Ed Hernon calculated they had come about two hundred
miles. All without loss of a single life or a single animal.

Which was pretty fair going in any wagon master's book.

And there had been no sign of Indians at all. Nary a one.

Not yet, at least. No smoke signals, no weird night cries.

The wagon train was no more than seventy miles from the borderline that dropped south to the Oklahoma Territory and rose northward to Kansas. A point where an important decision would have to be made by David Bard and the others, pending the wise advice of Fast Ed Hernon. The wide stretches of Missouri had been free of major challenges of any kind. Things had gone along smoothly, with no more than minor hitches. Rusty Hevelin had busted an ankle when his horse threw him, stepping into a gopher hole; five of the children had come down with fevers, but the womenfolk had seen them through that safely. Diane Sampson was with child, but the baby wasn't due for a long while yet. Nancy Wockenfuss and George Atkins, no more than twenty each, had fallen in love, and David Bard had performed his first marriage ever—on the trail, under the shade of a big hickory tree, close by a running stream. That had made everyone feel like a million U.S. Government dollars, and though David rued the private fact that Edna Sunset still wanted to wait, the camp was a festive place that night. And the bridal chamber proved to be the wagon of the Sampsons, who gladly gave up their bed for the night to the young 'uns.

What made David Bard feel all-fired wonderful was Edna's loving remark when the ceremony was over: "I saw Martinius marry a lot of people, David, and he never did it any better." It mattered to no one that David Bard

was not an ordained minister or true man of the cloth. The
company had accepted him as preacher and holy man. The
code of the West decreed no further judgment. It was the
recognized law of the community, just like picking your
own mayor, sheriff, and schoolteacher.

David that night never wanted Edna Sunset more. But
they could not meet. Everybody was awake and celebrat-
ing; the children in the wagon didn't want to go to sleep,
and it just wasn't possible. In truth, David and Edna had
not made love again since the night by the running stream
when they thought they had not been seen.

Fast Ed Hernon maintained his aloofness from all things.
Nobody questioned him or tried to draw him out—this
man who could shoot the head plumb off a rattlesnake at a
distance of twenty feet faster than you could say the word
snake. Or shout "Look out!" Not that anyone thought Fast
Ed Hernon was a mean man or an ornery cuss. It was
simply that they recognized his need for privacy, his bent
for not mixing with folks.

That too was his privilege and his right. But more than
one female in the camp, the widows and the unmarried
ones, cast coquettish eyes in his direction. After all, good
men were scarce and Ed Hernon looked like a good catch
for any woman. But there, too, he kept his distance. And
soon even the most forward of the ladies took the hint and
stayed away from him. Though Pam Adamson did all but
drop her drawers the night of the Atkins' wedding, down
by the stream, and only backed off when Ed Hernon wiped
her kiss from his mouth and stepped back with a tight grin
and said: "I don't care none for thin-lipped females. And
you've got thin lips, Ma'am."

So Fast Ed Hernon rode alone, always. And continued

to dream of a woman with cornflower-blue eyes, hair the color of ripe corn, and skin the texture of silk. David Bard's woman.

Who was woman enough to know and understand the curious manner in which Ed Hernon looked at her, eyed her, whenever their paths crossed during the long journey. She did not mention a word of her discomfort to David. She did not dare, sensing what his response might be. But Sister Edna Sunset was certain she could keep the situation in hand, if she minded her own business and made sure she was never left alone with Fast Ed Hernon. She erred deeply in her evaluation. She had underestimated a man who had always been able to do what he set out to do. What he had his mind set on.

This was a frontiersman who had kept himself alive once, snowbound in the Rocky Mountains, in a cabin that was without food, for fourteen whole days until his partner came back to bring him out in one piece. Hernon had fed on the leather of his boots and the frozen snow all around him. He was that kind of a hardy, single-minded individual. The very sort of man that was carving a home out of the vast wilderness of the American West. The pioneer stock, tried-and-true. A man who had also once been clawed by a grizzly bear and lived to tell the tale.

So Fast Ed Hernon trapped Sister Edna Sunset one late afternoon as the wagon train paused in the shadows of the river that not even he knew the name of. He only knew that Springfield lay some sixty miles due north. David Bard was in conference with Clear, Hevelin, Beigel, and Link Hullar, formulating a proper plan to ford that river. Hernon had offered his advice and experience and then withdrawn, for the fording would not be done until the

morning. It was then that he spied Sister Edna Sunset
down at the river's edge, filling a bucket from the clear,
rushing water. The river was not too wide across at this
point, a mere fifty yards, but it would be no picnic crossing the barrier. It was wagon-wheel deep and it would take
a lot of gumption and savvy to risk the fording. But it had
to be done, for not doing so would mean going miles
around the spot. About ten miles further along the stream.

"Sister Edna—need any help?"

"No, thank you, Mr. Hernon. I can manage."

"Looks mighty heavy, filled up like that."

"No matter. I've grown used to it."

He was on foot, as she was, leaving his sorrel to graze
freely. And despite his harmless words, there was that
undercurrent, that tone that said so much more than the
words. And that look in the dark brown, unblinking eyes.
She hefted the bucket, swung it to one side and tried to go
around him. He blocked her deftly. Almost as if by acci-
dent. She gazed past him helplessly. A high wall of bram-
ble bush screened them from the camp, but a hundred
paces away. Fast Ed Hernon didn't tower over her, but he
seemed to now.

"Please let me by."

"Can't we talk a spell? We hardly ever do."

"There's nothing to talk about, Mr. Hernon. Is there,
really?"

"I think so." His hands were on his hips, close to the
gun butts whose ivory handles gleamed in the dying sun-
shine. "You're not like the rest of the females, Sister
Edna. I know it and you know it."

She lost her uneasiness and eyed him in genuine surprise.

"Whatever are you talking about, Mr. Hernon?"

"You know what I'm talking about. That's what I mean. You're no fool. You know the way I been looking at you. You know what I'm thinkin' and what I'm feelin'. Don't you? Well—don't you?"

She nodded slowly, amazed at his forthrightness and yet still troubled. "I reckon I do. And if you know all that, then you also know why I've been avoiding you and keeping my distance, don't you?"

His smile, under the broad-brimmed hat, was somber.

"I do. David Bard. The preacher-man."

"Yes, that's right. David Bard."

"The preacher-man. But also no more than a boy. You need more than a boy, Sister Edna. You need a man. My kind of man."

"Please . . ." She made the mistake of trying to go by him again. "I mustn't listen to this." She came too close to him, and Fast Ed Hernon lost whatever composure and cool behavior he had foisted upon himself for these many weeks, for all this hungry, yearning time he had spent alone in the saddle and on the cool earth at night. Dreaming, fancying, imagining. His self-control melted away and he seized her roughly, pulling her to him. Before she could drop the bucket and defend herself, his moustached mouth had borne down on her swiftly. Burning, bruising, imploring for a return from her of the same wild, chaotic feeling. The same lust and love.

She did not struggle. She did not squirm. She clung to the water bucket, arms held downward. But she went cold, lax, none of her responding to the stolen kiss. Fast Ed Hernon could never be accused by anyone who had ever known him of being thick-headed. Her message, her answer, came across to him as if she had delivered a ringing slap to his bold face, as any other woman would have done. Any other woman who didn't want him. He released her, almost as suddenly as he had grasped her. He fell back, his face flaming with her rejection, his dark brown eyes furious with anger.

Edna Sunset tilted her chin.

"I hope you understand you are never to do that again."

He couldn't speak at first. He nodded almost dumbly.

"I won't mention this to anyone if you don't. I swear to that. It would only cause trouble."

"Go," he muttered, holding back words he didn't want to say, for he despised losers, whiners, and mollycoddles more than anything. "Go back with your water bucket. To that boy of yours."

"Thank you—I will."

He watched her take her leave, the tall, splendidly fashioned figure walking straight and proud back to camp. When the wall of brambles obscured her from his view, he cursed mightily, hating himself thoroughly for showing his hand before she had asked to see his cards. He had played very badly, and he loathed that more than anything. His hot blood had trumped him. Damn her—she was far too much woman for that greenhorn boy—a Bible-thumper, a Holy Joe, a goody-goody. Memory of Sister Edna Sunset's warm, sweet mouth and the full figure he had held for but a minute was too much for him. He cursed again and faced the rushing river waters.

Almost instinctively he spun his pistols out of their leather holsters with that lightning-swift frontiersman's draw. They appeared in his hands like magic. He stared down at them, shaking himself. His fingers tightened on the triggers until he relaxed his tug.

The brace of guns were Colt Navies, .36 caliber, and he suddenly remembered the day he had bought them in St. Louis, three years ago. The summer of eighteen hundred and fifty-six. He had killed more than a dozen men with them, and he remembered that too.

And by Christ, he'd kill one more, if he had to.

Even if it had to be a preacher-boy. A man of God.

He knew in his heart of hearts and soul of souls that he still wanted Sister Edna Sunset. Nothing was going to change that. He knew himself all too well. Two men, one woman. One of the men had to bow out or die—and it wasn't going to be Fast Ed Hernon. Not by all the fires in Hell. There was time enough to settle all this, once the trail drive was done. He couldn't kill David Bard, not now. Not with all the friends he had, the faithful following. But—a sudden gleam shone in Ed Hernon's dark eyes. Accidents did happen, didn't they? Or rather, they could happen. A dozen, different, innocent ways on a journey like this one. Why, hell, you could count on it, all things considered. The wagon train had been pretty lucky so far. No casualties, no really bad breaks. Who would be surprised if something awful were to happen after all this time? Even if it happened to the head man of the expedition. David Bard, the preacher-man himself.

He would never be anything but a boy to Fast Ed Hernon.

This despite the fact that he had very obviously already had the only real woman that Fast Ed Hernon had ever wanted. Sister Edna Sunset, a walking angel on earth. She glowed like the sunset.

Fast Ed Hernon strolled slowly back to his horse, pondering.

The dark eyes were lidded again. No one would know what his thinking was now, or where his true feelings lay. Or that murder nestled in his soul. Death for David Bard. Nothing else made sense, for Fast Ed Hernon. It was a man's way of settling his grievances.

"What are you thinking, Edna?"

"Of us, David. And what's to come."

"That's worth thinking about," David Bard smiled. "When I think about the future, I don't see nothin' in it but you, Edna."

"*Anything*, David—I don't see *anything*."

"There you go. Always correcting me. But you just keep on doing that. If a man's going to teach people how to live properly, it stands to reason he should talk right."

They were at the wagon, sitting on the driver's seat, close together. The night had come again. Peaceful, still. The moon, as big as a silver dollar, shone in the sky. The children were fast asleep and it was getting on to their own turning in. The camp had been a good one again. Horsefall's survivors had proven fine trail people. They had all made their necessary adjustment to homelessness, rootlessness, and wandering. The dream of a permanent home, a town of their own, at the end of this long, hard trail, had sustained them. As well as David's nightly readings to them from the Holy Bible, a book in which he was becoming more and more versed. He had a tendency to read with Martinius Rheinbeck's grand passion, but that was all to the good as far as Edna Sunset was concerned. It was somehow fitting that Martinius should live on in David Bard. It was another miracle of the Lord's.

Suddenly she closed her arms around him, her head

falling to his shoulder. "David, David, David . . ." she said his name with fervent longing. He hugged her, his face burrowing into the golden forest of her hair.

"Edna, you're shivering."

"It doesn't matter. You're here. Tell me again that you love me. Over and over again. I want to hear that so much."

"You know I love you," he said chidingly.

"Say it," she insisted. "Please."

"I love you, Edna. I love you."

Her mouth came up. They kissed. A powerful tremor coursed through her body. It was then that she realized how truly frightened she was. For herself, but mostly for him. Images of the bad scene on the riverbank with Fast Ed Hernon now filled her with desperation and tension. Forcefully, but gently, David pushed her from him. He searched her eyes, holding her by the rounded shoulders.

"Something's wrong. I know it, feel it. What is it, Edna?"

She shook her head, smiling to cover her uneasiness.

"It's just me, that's all," she managed a feminine sigh. "I want you again—so much—and we have to wait."

"*That*," he agreed ruefully, deceived by what she had said. "I hardly think of anything else; sometimes . . ."

"It'll be worth waiting for, David Bard," she promised with all the sincerity in her soul. "You just wait and see."

"I don't doubt that at all, Edna Sunset," he answered sadly.

They sparked in the shadows of the wagon seat as the children and the camp slept. The moon seemed closer than ever. As low as a treetop in the sky. Sister Edna Sunset shuddered once more, hoping with all her heart that no harm would come to David Bard.

But she could not quite wipe out what she had seen in Fast Ed Hernon's eyes when she had rebuffed him and he had talked about David Bard. There had been so much hate and scorn in his words. And cold fury in his frontiersman's face.

Edna Sunset, even as David held her in his arms, silently prayed, asking the Good Lord for his protection and sweet mercy.

She was somehow certain that David was going to need that mercy and protection before this long journey was done. She had little idea how right she would prove to be. The new day was to be a terrible one. Like nothing that had gone before.

SAVAGE SUNDANCE

At sunup, with breakfast seen to, the leaders of the camp set about making their plans for fording the difficult river. Richard Clear, Rusty Hevelin, and Andy Beigel had all agreed with David Bard and Fast Ed Hernon on the best spot to make the crossing. The water was at its lowest there, with heavy rocks breaking the surface and diverting the strength of the stream. Everything was set, and David was primed to take the Conestoga over first, when Fast Ed Hernon suggested one last check-over of the terrain. He claimed there might be a spot some one hundred yards down the bank which would be even simpler. David readily agreed, and he and Hernon set off on their reconnaissance. Sister Edna Sunet, knowing what she knew about Fast Ed Hernon, would have stopped them had she been present. But she was in the Sampson wagon seeing to Diane, who was in the third month of her pregnancy, and feeling poorly. Clear, Hevelin, and Beigel saw no reason to be suspicious of anything. As far as they were concerned, the preacher-man and the veteran frontiersman got on just fine.

They should have been suspicious.

Ed Hernon had indeed checked that point of the river some one hundred yards down the line. There the river grew more treacherous than ever. And with a blow with a gun butt to a man's head and a push into the racing current, there was no telling where the body would end up. For the rushing river was roaring in the opposite direction, away from the campsite. No one would see anything, and he would come back with the sad story of David Bard tripping, falling in, and being borne away with the tide before he could stop him. Nothing Sister Edna Sunset would say could change anything. Hysterical women who have lost their lovers would not carry much weight with the people of the camp, since neither by word nor deed had Fast Ed Hernon shown any malice or hostility toward young David Bard. In fact, he had done nothing but obey all his orders and keep in line since the start of this arduous trek across the wide open country.

"The water looks plumb worse here, Hernon."

"It quiets down a little further along. Wait and see."

"Hard to believe. That current seems even faster to me. Don't see how it could lessen unless there's a break in the riverbed."

"There must be. Looked pretty tranquil early this morning when I was out here to take another look around."

"All right. If you say so."

They pushed on, leap-frogging the falling-away shoreline with its rocky profile touching the water. Ed Hernon closed behind David Bard. The undergrowth lapping into the stream now concealed them both from the camp. With his right hand Hernon slowly and stealthily drew forth one of the Navy Colts. And raised it over his head for the stunning blow that was sure to topple the young preacher before him into the rushing river.

There was no sense left in his brain now, no rational thinking to keep him from a murderous, cowardly act—one that he probably would regret all the rest of his life. But the thought of Edna Sunset and possession of her and all that she was had blinded him to the ruthlessness of what he was about to do. He was past all reason, as if he were drunk with too much wine.

Yet, even as he brought the gun butt down in a murderous arc, David Bard whirled suddenly and the frontiersman was shocked to find the wrist of his gun hand caught in a vise more powerful than he could have imagined. And David Bard's blue eyes were but inches from his face. David Bard gritted out between his teeth the damning words: "No, Judas, not that way—if you're going to kill me, do it like a man. Face-to-face!"

"Damn you, Bard! I will!"

That ended all talk, all words, blocked any attempt at explanation or motives. Perhaps David Bard had known all along, had sensed this lonely man's hunger and the tension building throughout the long days on the trail. Whatever it was, he had saved his own neck at the last second and now he was going to have to save it again. Fast Ed Hernon dropped the Navy Colt and lashed out with a vicious knee. Upward. A killing blow. Into David Bard's groin. From that moment forward, the hand-to-hand encounter became a life-and-death duel, one which would certainly leave one of these men dead. If not both. It was now truly kill-or-be-killed, and no quarter for he who was down. And defenseless.

The savage knee missed David because he shifted with the speed of a striking rattler, caught the knee, and heaved mightily. Hernon cursed and fell back, catching himself before he fell into the river. David went for his own Navy Colt. But he had not reckoned with Fast Ed Hernon, veteran of a dozen saloon brawls and dirty fighter par excellence. The frontiersman came roaring back, butting his head like a bull, catching David in the stomach. Then Hernon closed in, following up the advantage, and in no time at all both men were locked together in a savage waltz of struggle. Bear-squeezing, clawing, scratching, punching. The morning sun, so serene and splendid, beat down, warming men who had no time for sunlight. Only punishment. And self-defense. It was a clash of Titans.

Hernon with his pioneer-hardened muscles was taken aback to find that the stripling in his grasp packed genuine muscle and whiplash energy. It was like trying to wrestle with a bear. The young preacher was a whole lot more than words and book-learning. Somewhere in his past he had learned how to fight and how to take care of himself. Hernon felt the taste of blood in his own mouth even as his hard eyes saw the threat of scarlet oozing down the preacher's cheekbone near the left eye. Ed Hernon growled exultantly. The sight of blood made him redouble his attack. But Bard would not yield, and now both struggling figures staggered and lurched perilously close to the water's edge. There was no thought of going for one's gun anymore. The enemy must be beaten with fists. A weapon would be superfluous and somehow degrading. Hernon felt

that now. David did too. There was a terrible urgency in
the air. A smell of death. It was as if the Grim Reaper
were watching from some vantage point as two men fought
each other for their lives. One of them for a woman and
position. The other from only a feeling of righteousness
and self-preservation.

And then the Bible got in the way.

And the Bowie knife.

Both possessions had had a curious history for David
Bard. The Bible had been his guide and comfort these last
hectic weeks. The Bowie knife had literally changed the
course of his life since that morning at Harpers Ferry.

Ee Hernon could feel the fight shifting now. With all his
force concentrated, his hard hands trying to beat David
back and down, he could tell he was losing. The youth
was simply too strong, too resourceful at close quarters.
There was no putting him off—the longer the struggle
lasted, the younger man was going to win. It was as sure
as Injun cruelty, as dead certain as the beauty of Edna
Sunset. Their breathing racked and labored, their locked
figures rocking at water's edge, the die was cast. David
Bard had achieved a hammerlock on Ed Hernon and was
bending him slowly and inexorably to the ground.

Fast Ed Hernon's instincts fused and exploded. Gone
was any pride and honor. A man had to win when losing
meant dying. So he went for his remaining Navy, clawed
it from its holster and pressed it directly into David Bard's
middle and fired. Point-blank, the closest range there can
be. The sudden thunder parted the combatants. And Fast
Ed Hernon was free at last, and David Bard was staggering
backwards, his eyes wide open in shock and surprise.
Staring dumbly, helplessly, down at himself. Knowing he

was a dead man even as he stared. Ed Hernon's dark eyes
flicked with pleasure and triumph. The fight was over and
he had won. No matter the low method he had used to best
this young preacher-man.

And then it was Fast Ed Hernon's turn to register shock
and surprise. The very last emotions of his action-packed
lifetime.

Something lanced into his back. Something awful.

Something rigid and firm and straight as an arrow.

For a mad second he was struck numb—frozen—and
then the sharp object went in deeper and deeper and he
cried out in agony, a hoarse scream erupting from his
lungs. And then he was falling, toppling, arms outstretched.
He plummeted into the racing river face-first, and the
gurgling, streaming current bore his bobbing, already-dead
body swiftly out of sight around the next bend of the river.
But the overhead sun glinted off the staghorn handle of the
Bowie knife jutting from his broad back. Driven in so deep
and far, it was sunk almost up to the hilt—a knife which
had come full cycle since the death of Corporal Raymond
Zimmerman.

David Bard saw the whole insane scene from a sagging
position at water's edge, one leg trailing into the river. His
hands were clasped to his middle, trying to stanch the flow
of blood that truly was not there and would not come. Fast
Ed Hernon's murderous shot had penetrated the worn copy
of the Bible which David Bard had tucked inside his
buckskin shirt that very morning, where he always carried
it so that it would not get damaged. But he did not realize
that yet. His mind, and his eyes, were far too stunned at
the sight of Sister Edna Sunset, her lovely face buried in
her hands, her shoulders heaving with sobs, standing like

an avenging angel on the rising ground above him. "Edna
. . ." The name came out of him in a moan. "Edna . . ."

At the sound of his voice, her hands flew from her face,
the cornflower-blue eyes popped in wonder and a relief as
dazzling as a noon sun. "David—oh, my God,—you're
alive—alive!"

It was then that his trembling fingers explored, remembering his Bible. His thumb found the chunk of lead which
had pierced the Good Book dead center, ruining it forever.
God's own miracle.

And Edna came scrambling down the bank, her arms
encircling him, helping him to his feet, steadying him, the
tears raining down her smooth cheeks. They held each
other for what seemed like an eternity. A moment that
would not come again. He was back from the grave and
Sister Edna Sunset had killed a man to save his life. Killed
Fast Ed Hernon with the Bowie knife he had somehow left
in the wagon that morning, without strapping it to his gun
belt.

"I knew he meant you harm—oh, David, I had to do
it."

"You saved my life—you and Martinius' Bible."

"When they told me you and he had gone walking, I
just knew he was going to try to kill you."

"How did you know, Edna?"

"It was the way he looked at me—the things he said—oh,
David—it was necessary, wasn't it? The Lord will forgive
me, won't he?"

"Hush, girl. Let's go back; we'll tell the others what
happened. They'll understand. They'll think you were bringing me my knife. They'll have to believe us or we're in
real trouble."

Even now, as he thought hard and quickly, he was
wondering why the sound of the shot going off hadn't
brought somebody on the dead run. He had the answer to
that almost before they started back for camp, his arm
looped about her shaking shoulder. His ribs ached with the
force of Ed Hernon's bullet which had slammed the Bible
into his flesh like a battering ram. But suddenly one shot
seemed laughable. A veritable fusillade of gun blasts sounded
from the direction of the campsite, where the wagons were
waiting to cross the dangerous river. Where all the others
were.

A bloodcurdling cry soared over the treetops, filling the
air. A coyotelike, shrill scream. But no mere coyote ever
had sounded like that. It was a man-made noise. The fierce
warrior cry of the red man on the warpath. Red men with
paint on their faces.

"Lord, Lord . . ." David Bard's blood chilled, the
blood that had been so hot only moments ago.

Edna Sunset shrank against him, her slender fingers
digging into his shoulder. "David—"

Dead or not, Fast Ed Hernon had been right, as usual.

The long-awaited, always-feared Injun raid had come at
last. In the full light of a clear morning, on the banks of a
rushing river, somewhere close to the border of Missouri,
at the very foothills of the Oklahoma Territory. Where few
white men had gone.

David Bard and Sister Edna Sunset ran back to camp, as
rifles cracked and war whoops went up, and horses whinnied in terror.

THE PROUD BROTHERS

There were nearly a hundred of them, hostile Indians on horseback, sweeping in from the hills, armed with rifles and their traditional bows and arrows. Galloping in a headlong cavalry rush, seeking to overrun the little encampment at river's edge. Six wagons and a group of men, women, and children, seemingly hopelessly outnumbered. But there was a difference this time. A major one. Richard Clear, Rusty Hevelin, Andy Beigel, Link Hullar, Bob Sampson, Frank Hamilton, Joe Lewandowski, Don Higgins, and their women and their children had all learned the lessons of the trail and the outdoor life full well. They had had the awful experience of Horsefall. And Horsefall was not going to happen again. These hardened settlers had now the wisdom of a prior experience. And also, there wasn't a man among them who wasn't a good shot now.

Horsefall's survivors also had David Bard, the young

preacher-man. And this day, ironically, David Bard's twentieth birthday, the inheritor of Martinius Rhenibeck's Bible and flock was to become a legend. A living legend who would be talked about and wondered at and marveled over for all the years to come. David Bard and the woman at his side, Sister Edna Sunset. They were to be giants who would live on long after the memory of Fast Ed Hernon was dust. And ashes, never to be recalled. This was not the war party that Hernon had dreaded. That band of vengeful Fox warriors, allied with other renegades, had not caught up with the wagon train. This attacking band was Osage—hardened red men eager to add to the scalps above their hunting lodges, anxious to add white squaws to their tribes and their tepees. So they bore tomahawks, scalping knives, and rawhide thongs with which to bind prisoners. And they would not return to their tepees empty-handed. That would bring shame on them before their own people. So it was to be a fight to the death. A massacre, if need be.

The terrible struggle began at a quarter to nine.

It did not end until hours later.

And all the time in between was marked by courage, heroism, and great feats of strength and endurance. And grand shooting.

David Bard and Edna Sunset reached the safety of the wagons just as the first charging wave of red men wheeled to a halt before the encampment, no more than thirty yards away. David quickly dispatched two with dead shots from his own Colt. From all the wagons rifles and shotguns poked, and these went off in a salvo, guided by Richard Clear's thundering command to fire in unison at the first onslaught. It was something to hear and see—at least a dozen braves fell from their horses, emitting death cries. The charge was broken and the Osage raced back to form another line, firing as they went. Link Hullar cried out in anger as an arrow buried itself in his left shoulder, but he ignored it and kept on blasting away with his rifle. His unerring eye accounted for another galloping Osage.

Dour-faced Andy Beigel, stationed below his own wagon, the muzzle-loader primed and ready, did not miss a single Indian he aimed at. The dead bodies began to pile up at the edge of the clearing. And then the Osage came dashing back in another furious charge, waving wildly, screaming their coyotelike battle cry. David Bard, all thoughts of Fast Ed Hernon and what had occurred on the riverbank that morning stored away for future consideration, now showed the leadership and daring of which he was capable. He mounted his strawberry roan, each hand holding the Colt and the horse pistol, the legacy of the swinish Tarzy brothers, and spurred his mount directly at the oncoming horde.

Their surprise and wonder at such bravery made them rein up their own horses and broke their charge. The single-action repeating pistols in David Bard's hands now went off in rapid firing. The immediate toll was staggering and thoroughly demoralizing to the attacking Osage. Horses bolted and skidded in alarm as their riders dropped like flies on a hot summer afternoon. And David was galloping back to safety before they could recover. The men in the wagons cheered lustily, the women clapped their hands. And Edna Sunset, frightened for David but resolute all the same, tugged the feathered shaft from Link Hullar's shoulder. He grinned his painful thanks and reloaded, his smooth face purposeful. The other wagons kept up a steady stream of rifle and pistol fire as fast as the reloading could be accomplished. The Osage were decimated by nearly half their warriors before an hour had gone.

So they gave up their charging and positioned themselves behind rocks, bushes, and trees to settle down to marksmanship and selective shooting, at which they all excelled. The hideous caterwauling had ended too. Now was the time for stealth and cunning. An Injun trickery. The wagons tensed. Ready for anything. And all the while, David Bard moved from wagon to wagon, crawling on his stomach beneath them, issuing instructions and steadying everybody as best he could. He was an example to all by sheer fortitude, not once thinking of his own hide or backing away from the situation. It was a situation that now assumed the proportions of a siege. The red devils were not going to go away, no matter how many warriors they had lost. And their marksmanship began to tell.

One of the wagons burst into flame as a shower of fiery arrows found the canvas front of the vehicle. There was a mad scramble by the occupants to douse the flames with water from the kegs lashed alongside, but this cost two lives—Ned Chase and Ward Tompkins, two farmers who had already lost their wives at Horsefall. They went down with Indian arrows sticking out of their chests. Edna Sunset cried out in horror and pity and then grimly raised her shotgun again. The wagon burst apart, smoking, flaming. And all the other wagons were far too close to one another—it was a setup that would worsen if something weren't done right away.

David Bard did that, too—something that took over more gumption.

Before anyone could stop him or think of what he could

be up to, he had sprung to the wagon, trundled it a good distance away, unhitched the defenseless horses, and come running back, surrounded by flashing arrows and puffs of dirt kicking up the sod where rifle fire missed his darting figure. Richard Clear shook his head in wonder, muttering, "He may be no older than a boy, but he's all man."

Rusty Hevelin, his cheek split wide open where a rifle ball had grazed him, spat a stream of tobacco juice in agreement. "That's our preacher, Richard. Reckon I'd die for him if I had to."

"Hope you don't have to, but Amen to that, Rusty."

The battle and the siege wore on. The children, frightened beyond comprehension, huddled close to their elders, trying to help any way they could, but there wasn't much children could do but be afraid. And help load the firearms. There weren't enough guns to go around as it was. Andy Beigel lamented the absence of some black powder or a firecracker or two. That would fix the wagons of these red hyenas, he vowed out loud. Bob Sampson, protecting Diane because of her delicate condition, laughed aloud at the suggestion. "What do you think this is, Beigel? The Fourth of July?" Andy shrugged and Diane Sampson smiled bravely through her fears. In Nick Carr's wagon, one more pioneer lay dying and there was nothing that could be done for him. Pat Dumony, a blacksmith from New York, had been mortally wounded, catching a rifle shot high in his thick chest.

The flaming arrows were their biggest fear now. For there was no way to stop them without exposing one's self to murderous Indian fire. David Bard, grime-faced, emotionally exhausted, tried to think of a way out of the dilemma. But one would not come. Unless—suddenly his eyes lit up. It struck him so forcibly that he almost erupted with laughter. All within sound of his voice and sight of him stared at him, afraid he had lost his mind under the stress of the battle. "David," Joe Lewandowski asked concernedly, "you all right, son?"

"The wagons, dammit," David Bard thundered. "The wagons! Why are we staying here—caught like rats in a trap! Drivers, mount up! Everybody aboard—we're going to cross that river while the crossing's good. Come on— move! The Good Lord helps those who help themselves. That's what it says in the Bible, and by God, we all are about to prove it! Mount up, I said!"

Bewildered, stunned, the sense and meaning of what he had just said penetrating all their clouded minds, the survivors of Horsefall and this latest onslaught of hard luck and tragedy did as he ordered them. David took the reins of the Conestoga, Edna Sunset at his side as always. He smiled back at the huddled children. "You keep your heads down now. There's bound to be a lot of firing when those red devils see what we're up to. But we'll make it. I swear to you, we will. Just be brave and pray."

From that moment the shooting from the wagons stopped and the first lead wagon, the heavy Conestoga, suddenly rolled forward, riding down the slight slope of the river-bank into the racing current to be followed in order by four other crowded wagons. The besieging Osage were taken completely by surprise. It was a miraculous sight. Five prairie schooners pushing across the rushing river, wheel-deep in the raging tide, wheeling on slowly but relentlessly to the opposite shore. The wagons swerved, tilted alarmingly, but the white fleet moved on. The Osage, reacting far too late, tried to follow on their mounts. But the river's rush and their lighter weight made the passage difficult. And the very few who dared to venture across were now at the mercy of Link Hullar's deadly rifle. From the last wagon, Link picked them off, one by one. As if he were in a shooting gallery and the Osage were so many clay pigeons. Link Hullar killed the pursuing braves with more pleasure than he had ever done before. His dead friends triggered his vengeful mood. Ned Chase and Ward Tompkins had been like fathers to him, not to mention the burly blacksmith from New York, Pat Dumony.

With great effort, the reins pulling at his raw hands as the horses fought the roaring water, David Bard's Conestoga wagon gained the far shore. He wheeled forward about twenty yards and swung the heavy wagon around, facing the shore from which they had just come. His heart filled with the sight of the other wagons all out of the river on dry land. Their drivers had followed his suit and a semicircle was formed. It was a grand spectacle, one to remember all one's lifetime. Particularly the view of the opposite bank of the river where the remaining Osage mounted, still armed, rode around in baffled circles not knowing what to do, seemingly. Until at last the foremost one raised his rifle in derision, emitted another fierce war whoop and then turned and finally galloped off, the other riders trailing in his wake. From all the wagons a great cheer went up. A long, heartfelt outburst marking grand joy and release from fright and tension. David Bard suddenly slumped wearily, letting go the ribbons. Edna Sunset put her head to his shoulder and said nothing. Nothing had to be said by her.

David Bard had not thought of Fast Ed Hernon since the first attack. No one else had, obviously. His disappearance had not been discussed by anyone during the battle. But now, with Ed Hernon's corpse floating down this racing river, maybe hung up on a rock in the stream or a dead branch sticking into the water—he would have to be discussed. A man just doesn't disappear. Not a man that you were last seen walking with—without somebody asking questions.

But amazingly, those questions were not to be asked. Not just yet, at any rate. During times of battle people are apt to overlook other people while they're protecting their own necks.

Richard Clear, Rusty Hevelin, and Andy Beigel were the first ones to hurry forward and extend their hands in admiration up to the young worn man sitting on the wagon seat, his face suddenly years-older-looking. The youthful innocence, the ingenuous smile, were gone. Possibly forever. Though twenty was not yet a man—legally, that is. David had decided to tell no one it was his birthday. Not even Edna Sunset. What a birthday. It was a day marked by slaughtering Osage.

Clear's benign face was wreathed in a marveling smile.

"You're a caution, Preacher." He couldn't call this giant David now. Not after all he had done. "You did right fine. Better'n any man I ever knew. Thanks to you, we're all safe again."

"I didn't do it all." David's smile was wan. "We've got some good shooters in this outfit. I saw Link Hullar pick off quite a few of those painted buzzards."

Rusty Hevelin squinted. "We couldn't have swung it without you. And that's a fact." Andy Beigel nodded and winked broadly.

"We got some more dead, Preacher," Clear said, break-

ing the mood. "Six more. And that just about leaves
maybe twenty of us."

"I know. We'll bury them here. By the river. To mark
the spot. Frank Hamilton will do the honors again, though
I suspect he wishes he didn't have to." Richard Clear
frowned. And shook his head.

"Can't be done. Frank took an arrow in his right arm.
His drawing arm—unless Andy here—"

"I'll do it," Andy Beigel said quietly. "Be an honor."

That settled that. All but the matter of Fast Ed Hernon.
And the business this morning at the riverbank up ahead.

David Bard opened his mouth to speak, but before he
could, Richard Clear held up both arms and spread them
out.

"If you're going to tell us about Hernon, forget it,
Preacher. We're none of us blind. We all saw how he was
setting his mind on Sister Edna. It was as clear as sunup to
every one of us. You were too busy with the books to
notice. I knew he took you for that walk because he
wanted to have it out with you. Didn't figure it would get
out of hand, though, until I saw Sister Edna go running off
after you with that Bowie knife hugged to her. I was about
to take a look, and then those Osage showed up—"

Rusty Hevelin coughed, interrupting, fingering his red
beard.

"You see, we knew this spot was the only place to
cross. Hernon's fish story didn't fool us. But we also
figured you two had the right to settle your differences.
With fists or talk."

"So we don't want to know," Andy Beigel finished off
their confessions. "If he's gone forever, that's good enough
for us. Never cottoned to him much. A man that has no

time to talk to children or make them things, I haven't
much use for."

Edna Sunset's fingers pressed David Bard's arm. He
nodded and looked down at the three wise men fate had
thrown him in with. His smile now was affectionate as
well as grateful.

"It's mighty kind of you all to say what you have. To
trust me so much that you'll take my word on anything.
But you have a right to know—no, you *must* know what
happened out there this morning so there's nothing secret
between us. I think Edna Sunset would want you to know,
too—so I'm going to tell you."

And he did, sparing none of the details. He showed
them the copy of the Bible with Fast Ed Hernon's bullet
still imbedded in the cover. All through the recital Sister
Edna Sunset watched their friendly faces, looking for the
first sign of disappointment or reproach. There was none
of either. David could have lied for her, but she never
would have wanted that—something she had sensed he
would know. He was more and more like Martinius
Rheinbeck every passing day. Lies were not the way to
Truth and Salvation—not for this man she loved with all
her heart.

When David had finished, Andy Beigel grunted: "Like
I said, I never liked him. Good riddance."

Rusty Hevelin and Richard Clear exchanged understanding glances. Clear put his hands together. "That settles it,
then. We'll say no more about it. Personally, I would have
cheered had I been there to see you do it, Sister Edna."

"Hear, hear," Hevelin took off his hat and bowed in a
most courtly manner. "A woman who fights for her man
gets my vote. God bless you, Edna Sunset."

She was overcome by their reaction. They did not censure her or blame her or even vulgarize the truth of the thing—that she was David Bard's woman. They must have seen that, too, in all these long days on the trail. She and David had not fooled anyone!

She blushed. A full blush. From cornflower-blue eyes to the tip of her well-shaped chin. The men all smiled, nodding approval.

"Prettiest lady I ever did see," Andy Beigel murmured and limped off.

Clear and Hevelin were agreed that the wagon train should take a breather here, get some food into everybody, bury the dead, and then push on the next day. David Bard was of the same mind on that score. But before they left, he reminded them once more of something that could not be forgotten, that had to be remembered.

"When we cross over the Missouri line into the Oklahoma Territory, I want you two to keep your eyes peeled for the first decent place that strikes you. For settling down. We can't keep on like this. Another raid and there might be nobody left. The Good Lord has seen us this far. Let's not be asking him for too much help. You know land—you choose the spot—and there we'll stop the wagons and get out and start building. Shacks, then a barn—and then a church. For all of our souls."

Richard Clear smiled the broadest smile.

"You're the preacher, David Bard. Come on, Rusty. Let's see to those dead ones and the wounded."

"Right with you, Richard."

The sun was ascending again. It was almost high noon now. Edna Sunset gazed into his eyes, trying to read what she saw there.

"What are you thinking, David?"

David Bard drew her toward him, his face dirty but shining with an inner glow. The scraggle of beard had deepened into shaped formation so that now he truly looked like a preacher. A minister.

"I'm thinking how lucky we are to be alive and how much I love you, Sister Edna Sunset."

That, he knew with every ounce of his being, was something that was never going to change. Not for a single moment of his life.

Like the Lord himself, and the Good Book, the rightness and goodness of Edna Sunset was never going to leave him.

Neither the Lord, or the Good Book, or Edna Sunset.

She touched his grimy face and her eyes were glowing.

"Kiss me, David Bard. Please."

He did. In full sight of the camp, the world and all of the clouds in the blue sky above. The sun seemed to blaze down more intensely.

There was no turning back from God or the Bible or Love now. The road was fixed for him, the path set, the way showing clearly up ahead. He had brought the flock into the wilderness and kept them from harm and annihilation. The flock would live on.

World without end, Amen.

COME, ALL YE FAITHFUL

It was December, The second day.

A fateful month in the year of our Lord, eighteen hundred and fifty-nine. The furor in the nation which had spread like wildfire over the question of slavery in America had reached an apogee of concern. John Brown was to hang for his rash Harpers Ferry raid. And the country was divided over that gallows walk of the ex-Ohio farmer who had carried his abolitionist's fervor too far for any turning back now. The North had tried to have him freed; the South tried just as hard to have him hanged. At his trial, Old Osawatomie Brown had conducted himself with bravery and intelligence, making it difficult for all observers to believe he was the impassioned madman who had stormed an arsenal with but a handful of loyal, devoted followers. But the jury was adamant.

*. . . of the charges of treason against your country, you
are convicted, John Brown. . . .*

Hanging was the verdict, as payment for the crime.

Ralph Waldo Emerson, the poet, had already submitted
to print the thought that Brown would make his day on the
gallows "glorious as a cross." There was to be no record
as to how Walt Whitman felt on the subject, though doz-
ens of others expressed themselves very strongly in the
matter. John Brown had become the nation's conscience,
putting into solid form all the arguments about slavery, pro
and con. Yet the gallows did not wait—and John Brown's
bearded head fit neatly into the hangman's noose. People
cursed and people cheered all over the country. But the
lanky figure dangling at the end of a rope would cast a
longer shadow than any he had while alive.

A shadow that would bloom, blossom, and flower into
an ugly black cloud that would one day erupt into a civil
war.

John Brown's Body was never to be forgotten.

Soldiers young enough to be his sons would sing about
it.

Yes, the man was dead. Stone dead.

But his soul would go marching on.

The news did not reach the Oklahoma Territory until
three weeks after the execution by hanging. It traveled by
newspaper, by Wells Fargo stagecoach, by rail—by word
of mouth. A teamster told a barkeeper; a dance hall girl
told a customer—a traveling whiskey drummer—and ultimately, the story reached the territory, was dropped off by
a wagon train of settlers passing through on their way to
California. The wagon train halted at the little settlement

of Bardsville, where there was a dirt street of frame houses, barns, outhouses, and even a church. A tiny building with a wooden cross set back from the rest of the structures. Bardsville was no more than a jumping-off place, but it was a town. A point of civilization in the untamed wilds, and it looked like it was still growing. The wagon train was welcome to the water in the wells, and there was no end to the hospitality shown the trail people by the women and children of Bardsville. The menfolk enjoyed a pipeful and a chaw of tobacco with each other while they talked about life, the West, and what had happened to John Brown. When the news reached the little church at the end of the street, the Reverend David Bard and Sister Edna Bard paused at their daily study of the Holy Bible and looked at one another. Edna Sunset Bard now knew the fully story of her David's association with Brown. When Richard Clear had married them in his position of mayor of Bardsville, her new husband had told her all of his past. And now the past had come back again. Full force, like a blow to the face. But Martinius Rheinbeck's protegé, who had wanted to call this settlement *Rheinbeck*—he had been overruled by one hundred percent because of the things he had done in Missouri—was not sad at all. In fact, there was a placid smile on his handsome face which still showed a trim brown beard.

"You're not disturbed by the news, then, David?"

"No. Can't say that I am. I thought I might be. But I'm not."

"That's very strange, David, I must say. You were willing to die for that man once."

"I was. But that was before a lot of things and a lot of people. Like Martinius Rheinbeck, like you—and like God."

"Then I'm glad, David."

"I am too, Edna. It lifts a great load from my mind. I do feel sorry for John Brown. He was right about slavery, only wrong about his way of putting an end to the blight."

"Shall we say a prayer for him at mass on Sunday, David?"

"Yes, but a silent one. I don't think our congregation ought to start arguing among themselves about slavery, though the Lord knows it's an ugly, evil thing."

There was no more to be said now that she knew how he felt. She looked at him with loving eyes. He was so tall and straight now, with his Bible in his hand. Not even the gun butt still poking from his side could make her feel any differently, though she realized all too well how necessary a firearm was out here in the middle of nowhere. God's country, yes, but there were still wild Indians, bad white men and thieves and cutthroats and bandits. Religion was needed, right enough, out West, but the man who delivered that religion sometimes had to do it at the point of a gun.

As her David did. And was doing.

David Bard. A man of whom all Bardsville was proud.

Her husband. A good man.

A man of whom Martinius Rheinbeck would have been prouder still. Edna Sunset Bard sighed, turning the pages of her Bible to Exodus. The story of Moses the Prophet leading his people out of Egypt across the sands of the desert to a new home—as David had certainly done. If Martinius had only been alive to see it—but the Lord had seen fit to do things his way. It had not been meant to be. Sister Edna Sunset Bard was the true Christian in her ways. God ordained everything, including her love for

David and his love for her. It had been written that it should be so between them.

"Edna."

"Yes, David?"

"Do you still have that scrap of paper that man Whitman gave you back there in Kentucky?"

"Of course I have. I'm never going to lose that. It's such a lovely piece of writing."

"I think I'd like to read it Sunday. It's the sort of spiritual piece that would set well with them, I think."

"All right, David. I'll remember to give it to you."

He crossed to her then, putting aside his own book and taking her two hands in his own. He looked into the cornflower-blue eyes, saw the long, golden hair and his heart was full again. She in turn saw the face of a man she would always adore. He was so handsome, so forthright, so *good*.

"Do you still love me, Edna Sunset?"

"Edna Sunset Bard, if you please." Her eyes glowed. "Always, David. Forever and a day."

"That's a long, long time, Edna," he smiled.

"And that's just how long it will be then."

They embraced, clinging to one another. In their own church, in their own town, in their own refuge in the wilderness that was the West. Where their religion would be the bulwark which would sustain their love. And their people. The people of Bardsville.

The fastest-growing little community in the Oklahoma Territory. Bar none. No matter the troubles, the hardships, the tragedies looming on the country's vast horizon.

David Bard had found his calling in life.

The one that had probably been planned for him all

along, as far back as the cradle and when he was a babe in his mother's arms. Seeing the light of the world for the very first time, hearing a bird chirp from the nearby trees. Feeling the soft touch of his pillow, smelling the good clean air of living.

David Bard, the preacher-man.

Martinius Rheinbeck's prodigal son, indeed.

Born Catholic, yes, but now a spiritual man for all people.

Belief in the Good Lord was all that really mattered.

In the beginning and in the end.